*Codex of the Nine: The Crownless King*
by Jorge Vazquez

Published 2015 by The Light Network
Copyright © Jorge Vazquez

Printed in the United States

*Interior layout by Christi Koehl*

*Edited by Keidi Keating*

ISBN: 978-0-9966403-0-5

# CODEX OF THE NINE:
# THE CROWNLESS KING

By Jorge Vazquez

# ACKNOWLEDGMENTS

There are many trials we must face in life, and few can be accomplished without the aid of others. The moment I decided to conjure the story within my mind, I found myself merely doing so as a pastime. However, those closest to me believed the story could amount to more than just a hobby, thus inspiring me to reach for greater heights.

Andy, you are like a brother to me, I will never forget the good advice that you gave me so many times when I was close to falling down a bad path, for that I will be ever grateful, brother.

Nuray, my dear mentor, you are a blessing in every aspect of the word, and through your teachings I have grown both mentally and spiritually. Namaste.

While on a deployment, I had the support of many people such as Daniel, a good man who had much sound advice to give. You once said, "What would you like to change, the world or your world?" I still don't have an answer, but I believe that my life will speak for itself.

Steven, you once told me, "Just because you are capable of doing something does not mean you should." My friend, thank you for those simple yet true words, which I will always reflect upon.

Lawrence, you are full of inspiration and have always advised me to seek out life and culture. Thanks to you, I have seen a side to history otherwise fogged from my eyes.

Carlos, you are a true king in your kingdom. I thank you for being an honest man who allowed me to think outside of the norm.

Alan, over time you have proven to be both a good friend and a person with life experience worth a book itself. You have all been very supportive through endless hours spent on creating the book, and for that I am very grateful.

But the person who triggered the depth within the story, the one who brought about the Ashen curse to my mind was Hefzi. She is the sole reason the story truly came about. Because of you I have been able to bring to my mind a world with true life and passion, all serving as a testament to what an amazing woman you are.

I would also like to thank, Jesus, a good man who has been a vital part of my life, and one of the people who influenced my thoughts since my youth. It is because of you that I have become the man that I am today. You were both my best friend and like a father to me, for that I will always be grateful. Also, know this brother, you are a great inspiration for the stories I create, because you of all people have proven and displayed true chivalry, in a time that has little knowledge of such a thing.

Amalia, you cultivated deep thoughts as I grew up and have always been an amazing woman, who has believed in me from the beginning.

Jorge, thank you for the harsh lessons that have made me a strong man, and for your support through many hard times. With that strength I have been able to create this story.

Nancy, I thank you from the bottom of my heart, you are an amazing woman and I want you to know that Dionisio, your father, is the man I wish to mirror, and the one who told me to write a book, which now has led me to this point in my life.

Yexi, we lost so many years, but I am happy to say time has not yet ended.

Beyond those I have mentioned, I also have great appreciation for Ana and Laura for their support.

Finally I would like to say thank you to Stacy, David, and Kassandra, for supporting me and always believing in me.

The world lays in ruin. Every corner of this barren wasteland shouts in agony; the pain of all the people's lives can be seen within the ashes that cover the land. Once great kingdoms stood where I now stand, once men of great power dreamed of a better future; but now all of their hopes and dreams have scattered to the winds with the ashes of the fallen.

Some say it was a single man, others say it was a great war, but in truth what little is left of us, of humanity, is testament to our loss. Oftentimes legends are told to paint the beauty of what we desire, yet the truth is never so clear. As I walk, I can see the shadows of the past, their struggles and their passions, each person bearing a dream, each with a faith, and each with a story. My name is Gabriel. I was born in a time when the azure sky seized to exist. It is now a darkened gray, for the ashes of the fallen have blotted out the sky. There are no longer great kingdoms, no legends, no honor, no love; everything has long since withered along with the truth they had.

My father left many years ago when I was but a child, and mother was left alone in tears, awaiting his return. However, never did he make his way back to our home. Instead, she was condemned to die by those who called themselves the Wise Men. They were the leaders of this land, men who feared the past, and condemned any who meddled with it. Mother told many stories of the past; she spoke of a great king, who she said was called the king of kings, the ruler of all. In her stories, this king would face the horrors of a dark past that cast its shadow upon the lands, but with his might he would vanquish all the evils of the land. I, however, questioned this truth, as their world had ended in tragedy. Where was such a king when his people needed him the most? Where stood humanity's beacon of light?

Without an answer, she would stare at the sky and smile, but soon her smile was forever taken from my eyes, for the Wise Men took her from this life. Enraged, I fled to the fields of Ash where I came across

Lucian, an old man claiming to have known my father. Lucian, a man who came from their time, called to me, speaking in riddles of a possible way to save them, of a chance to change history. And in this chance, I would have to use the Codex to live what they lived, in the hopes of correcting their wrongs.

Handing me a letter, I gazed upon the written words. Not knowing whether I felt anger, grief, or joy I began to read.

*To my son Gabriel,*

*When you read this letter you shall feel confusion, hate, sadness, and curiosity. There is little time to console you, my son, nor can I ask you to forgive me for leaving our home as I did. But I hope that what I leave you with allows you to realize that sometimes one must do things that cause us more pain than a thousand deaths, but that it must be done for the greater good.*

*I have found what little history was left of the days when dreams and ideals had come to the lands. I attempt to piece together the mystery behind what brought about the end of an era, giving birth to a new one. A part of me believes it was the gods themselves that reigned terror upon man; for all that they had done in the dark days. However, history can be like the lights in the sky, which are merely there as a reminder of the Creator's existence. All is left to perspective. Whether it is the faith of history or the truth of it, I shall read through these archives left to me by the old king until I find the truth, for that is what he told me to do before he brought me to this time. That old king, who rescued me from the ignorance of the dying city, would ask of me what I now ask of you: to save them.*

*Mankind searches for something in life, something that lingers deep within the mind, something that slowly cultivates itself into a dream within the heart. Some seek salvation, others retribution, and some walk down a path with no purpose other than to live. It is said that within the darkest of times comes the brightest of minds, and as the skies darken some shall rise to meet the challenges that come. I believe that you, my son, have the fire that is needed to finish putting together the past so that we can save the future. The book that you now possess has the first piece of the truth. I will give you some insight so that you understand a bit of what you will be diving into.*

*There once was a kingdom of beauty and freedom, a place where all* could speak what truths they believed and where oppression was but an unfathomable thought. However, with such purity came envy from those who still lingered in the Ash ages. The Ash age was a time when war was waged against a kingdom and with its destruction an army rose from the ashes of the burning kingdom. They would be called the Ashen. Kings quivered in fear as the massive army of Ashen devoured the land like a plague.

Leading the armies was a knight of pure black armor, and with a single raise of his hand, his army would march with conviction. They marched from the north to the west, and then to the south burning everything in their path. Leaving the east to tremble before their might, the Ashen surrounded the kingdom; but as all hope was lost, the times sided with what was left of humanity as an unknown man walked into the Ashes, and in a flash of light was gone, along with the Ashen.

All that was left were those who fled to caverns, as all four kingdoms had fallen. From this day forth, the east built the south and the west, but the north was left in rubble as a reminder of the horrors it had brought. Some say that the northerners had become corrupt and this had led to the devastating Ashen war. With the lust for power came endless wars, and with these wars came a time of darkness that would breathe life to the end of all life. Wars were fought for power but men would masquerade them with words of faith. Thousands would give their lives for ideals that were mere illusions of what they so desired.

Never forget, Gabriel, each person is like a stone, and with every passing moment we are shaped by the people we love, those we hate, and those who we may never see. You see, they carry the hammer and chisel that gives form to the statue we ultimately become. The events that transpire in our lives are enigmatic and limitless. There are no rules as we are free to create what reality we so desire. Take these words and hold them close, for there will be dark days ahead of you, my son. But do not worry, for the man who is aiding you will make sure that you are able to walk this path without harm coming to you. It may seem too much too soon, but never forget that time passes and it never waits for us, so we have but one choice and that is to move with time, so that our lives can be more than mere stones.

By nature we are fueled by greed, lust, and pride, and we are damned to follow the path of war. Some refer to us as chaos in physical form, and *most say we are the bringers of death upon the world. But humans are also loving, compassionate, and full of potential for great things. Just because we are born with the stigma of our nature does not mean we can't stand away from the shadows and break away from the chains that bind us to our fate. There once was a man who stood before the Creator, right before the end and questioned His resolve. The man turned on the one who created him, all to save those he loved. His words echoed through the infinite, as the world burned, and everything turned to ashes. The Creator allowed him to live so that he could hold on to the ashes of all that he held so precious. For a thousand years the flames burned as the man kneeled in the ashes of all that he loved, so that he could remember his sin. Until the day the rain came once again, the man stood and walked into the darkness, never to look back, and he swore revenge upon the Creator. Our world was forever cut away from the heavens for we are all the descendents of this man. However Gabriel, I believe you can find the truth beyond the legend. Simply follow the path to the North where the man was said to have questioned the Creator. There you will find the truth, and there you will know who we are and what our purpose is. But before you go, take this book for it is one of the three books that hold the secrets of the past.*

*There is not much else I can tell you, my son. Time has not sided with me, but we will meet again...this I swear.*

*I love you, Gabriel*

Walking down the field of Ash as they call it, I held the Codex, an ancient relic that holds the memories of the past. I can see a great battle, not in this time but in theirs. I can see the sorrow in the lifeless faces of those consumed by the fires of war. In the center of this great battlefield laid scattered with the bodies of countless men, there kneels a knight bearing black armor. Looking up at the sky, all of the bodies slowly turn to ash. The ashes slowly cast themselves onto the black knight, turning his armor an ashen color. Here I can see the destiny of man, once creatures of great potential, and now mere ashes that scatter to the winds.

Looking upon the Knight, I walk, but as I come closer he says, "Don't come any closer; they take me, those from the Ashes of what I have done."

But as I stand still I feel a great sorrow, a great love, and a great loss emit from this knight. The ashes of the fallen continued to devour his being. Feeling compassion, I walk forth, and the closer I walk the more I feel his loss. Such pain…no man should endure this pain. Slowly I see what seem like his memories. Turning to me, I see not a knight but a king, a man with the eyes of defeat. He walks closer to me. "Bring them back; the nine are our only hope."

Looking at the Codex, I open it, and as I do everything around me begins to fade. Slowly I see the world around me disappear. As the world turns empty, I stand in nothingness, and I hear an old man's voice call to me.

"Gabriel, thou has called upon me. I am Codex, keeper of life. Speak, what does thou desire?"

"What my father desired. To change the past."

"The past may never change, but thou may witness it."

"Let me see. I wish to see them—the nine."

"Thou shall lose consciousness within the eyes of the nine."

"Then let it be so."

In a flash I see vast lands with forests, mountains, and beautiful clear skies. Soon I am drawn to what looks like Kingdoms, one made of gold, another of stone, and one of steel.

"Codex, what is this? Where am I?"

"Thou has stepped into the world of the nine to peer into the history of the fallen. Alluvium, a kingdom of gold, honor, and pride stands where the sun rises, as a beacon of hope. At the end of the day, the sun dies at the edge of the steel walls of Minaria, with those who too have become as cold as their walls. Looking down from those two kingdoms are the simple stone towers of Stein's Fortress, an old kingdom with much mystery engraved in its stones. Yet of all the kingdoms, none is more beautiful than Bartholomaois, once the most beautiful of all, yet you shall know it as the ashen covered husk, hidden from all to the north, forgotten and left to wither away."

"These are the four kingdoms of their time? Tell me Codex, what do I do now?"

"Your story begins in no such kingdom."

Suddenly I found myself standing in front of an enormous gate. I looked before me to see a kingdom, one such as the books mother had told me of, built of stone and wood, with walls that reached beyond the trees. Stretching for miles, it seemed endless. This was fascinating. One second I was in a field of ash holding the Codex, while I stood before a knight, and now I stood before a kingdom. Was this a dream or was this reality? Where was I, and what was I doing here? Looking behind me I saw a man wearing dark steel armor with an enormous sword, long black hair held up in a ponytail. His face was young yet his piercing green eyes showed many more years. His tanned skin was covered with dirt, and the dark armor looked cracked, as if he had just come from a battle. Walking next to him was another man who stood far taller than him, his size matched by his muscular physique. The other man seemed to only have leather armor and two swords. Walking closer to me, I extended my hand as if to stop them, but as I did they walked right through me.

The man in black armor turned back as if looking at me and said, "Zangar, did you feel something?"

Looking back, the man in leather armor said, "Nigh, you always have the strangest things to say. Maybe it was a bee. Let's go, it's getting late."

*What was that?* I said to myself.

"You are not of this world, merely an image to watch," said the voice of a woman.

"An image? What do you mean? Who are you?"

"I am Codex, the keeper of humanity's unfolding story, and you're here as a witness to its failure."

"Codex? Wait, that was the name of the book I just had in my hands. Are you a book?"

"I am merely a manifestation of what humanity could understand, if only to briefly coexist within your reality. I can be earth or sky, sun or moon, anything that man could fathom, so that I may exist."

"I've heard that the world came to an end through war but I still can't believe this to be real. Why am I here to watch humanity's failure?"

"Because only a human can judge a human. None shall hear your voice, none shall know of you, but you shall follow those who reached out to the sky, the nine who wrote the end of humanity's story."

"Before I came to this place I saw a knight who said to bring the nine back."

"Merely an image of the tormented fool who clings to the inevitable."

"I don't know what to say. What do I do?"

"Close your eyes; do you feel the presence deep within you? Follow that presence and you shall begin your journey. Tread carefully for those who you shall watch can consume you entirely, Gabriel, for you shall watch the world through their eyes."

Closing my eyes I heard the voice of the woman echo along with the voice of the old man, fading as it said, "Listen to their hearts for the truth." Opening my eyes I felt different, as if inside something. Before me laid a boy with black hair, olive skin, and dark brown eyes, wearing torn clothes as if he had nothing else. He laid on the rooftop of a wooden house, in what looked like a small village, with a few wooden houses. With his arms crossed behind his head, as he looked at a kingdom, the boy smiled. Walking inside the house was a tall thin man who looked just like the boy. Suddenly I was pulled closer to the boy. I felt as if I were being trapped, and with a burst of images I saw an entire life flash before me. I could see myself running with a woman I knew to be my mother, and a man I knew to be my father. Then the woman lay in the arms of the man as his hands were covered in blood, screaming in pain. I could see myself falling. It seemed these were the memories of another. I heard them call to me.

"Orion, come, let's go." Suddenly the flash brought me to a midday sight as the sun hid behind the trees.

# CHAPTER 1

## ORION DREAMER OF THE DAY

*It is the year 1109 when a war broke out with a group called the Blood Hand*

So it begins on a late afternoon, when the sun seemed to rise midway, staring at Stein's Fort, the kingdom of the southern lands, from the roof of my house. I admired its rough surface, as each wall was built of dark stone. I could see the roofs of the wooden houses in the distance where they stood at small hills. Smoke came out of the chimneys, and I could faintly hear people laughing, and kids like me, playing. I thought to myself, *One day I'll join the knight academy, and make everyone proud. One day I'll have my own wooden house with my father, and I won't have to lay here wishing I could be there.*

Sitting there by myself I heard my name. "Orion, hey Orion, get down from there." Looking to the side I saw Aleya walking closer. She had her long brown hair down, unlike most days, and wore a white dress that made her tanned skin stand out. I could see her waving at me, as her honey colored eyes shone with the sunlight.

She had moved to the south from a village near Alluvium, the kingdom of the east, a few years ago to try and live a new life with her mother and father, but it did not seem to go so well, since they were unable to work for the south's farmland due to the father's physical disability, having no function of his legs. Aleya had no friends, so she would always try and spend time with me. Father always told me to be nice to her because she had no friends, so I often tried to spend some time with her.

Walking closer to the house she asked me, "So I heard it was your birthday yesterday. You just turned ten and didn't say a word to me or Leon! Why?"

I shrugged my shoulders. "Sorry, I guess it slipped my mind."

Squinting as if suspicious of me lying, she ran to the side of the house where she could climb to the roof. Looking over to Leon's house I could see him peeking through the window. His pale skin and black hair was hard to miss. He looked upset as his blue eyes watched Aleya climb. Leon was my best friend since I could remember, but after Aleya arrived he changed with me, and started to distance himself. I never understood why he acted that way with me, even more so when she came around. But I no longer needed to know, as if he didn't want to be my friend then I understood.

Finally making it to the top of the house she sat next to me, looking at the kingdom with me. She said, "You always sit up here looking at the kingdom. Why?"

With a smile I said, "Because one day I'll join the knight academy, and have the strength to help others. I'll have my own sword, and I'll know how to fight."

Aleya looked at me. "So you need a sword, and to know how to fight in order to help people?"

"Yes, because if you're weak the world will punish you for it, which is why becoming strong is the only way to help others," I said as I thought of my mother's loss.

Aleya smiled at me and held my hand. "You already are strong, Orion. You help your father and everyone in the village. I don't think you need a sword to be strong. My dad used to practice medicine before his accident and he saved many lives. He never wielded a sword in his life and he still saved many."

Moving her hand off me I told her, "It's not the same! He could only save those who came to him; he couldn't reach out to the other kingdoms and help others. What I want is to be able to reach out to all the kingdoms and help all the people who need it."

With wondering eyes she said, "Orion, only a king can do all that."

"Exactly Aleya, only a king can do that, and that's why one day I'll be king of the south."

Aleya sat in silence, "You want to be king? But I thought you said you wanted to be a knight?"

All her questions aggravated me so I stood up, "Only a knight can be king, and why be a king if you can't even save lives with your own two hands?! I'll not hide in my throne while everyone dies for me; a true king knows how to fight."

Aleya sat in silence as I climbed down from the roof. She stared at me in confusion, but it did not matter because she would never understand.

Walking inside the house father surprised me with a short sword. "Orion, look what I got for you," he said with a smile.

My face lit up with surprise. "Is that real?"

Laughing he said, "Yes, now you must promise to be careful. I'll teach you a few things tomorrow morning."

Grabbing the sword from his hands I looked at him and asked, "You want to teach me? But how dad? You're just a farmer."

After I said that he looked serious. "Hey now Orion, I'm not just a farmer. I had a friend who became a knight a long time ago, and he made sure to teach me how to use a sword."

After he told me that, I wondered why he hadn't saved mom when she had been attacked. "Dad, if you knew how to use a sword why didn't you protect mom?" Father's eyes opened up. Standing in silence, he took a deep breath, and said with a sad voice, "Go to your room."

Walking to my room, I heard him crying. I felt sad for his pain but that made me angry. *This is what being weak does to people. Father could not save mother so now she's gone forever.* Lying in bed I cried in her memory, but it had been so long, and I was so young that I could not even remember her face. As I laid in bed I looked to the door of my room and noticed what seemed to be a knight standing in the shadows. In disbelief I closed my eyes and when I opened them again the knight was no longer there. Wiping the tears from my eyes I stood from my bed. Walking closer to the door I looked around and there was nothing strange. *I need to sleep. I must be tired after all this thinking.*

The following day I woke up with a heavy feeling. I knew that father and I had gone to bed on bad terms so I didn't know what to expect. But as the thought crossed my mind father walked in with a smile and the sword in his hand. "Orion, today we'll start your training. Let's go. Get off the bed." Father seemed to be excited to teach me. It seemed like he would always smile no matter how bad things got. I quickly gathered my things and rushed outside to meet him in the backyard.

Walking outside father stood holding two wooden swords. He looked at me with a serious gaze. "Orion, when we step in this place you must not see me as your father but rather your mentor." Walking closer he threw the wooden sword at my feet, and when I went to grab it he quickly struck my hand. "Always keep your guard; your opponent will use whatever he can to best you." Grabbing the sword, I rushed father with everything I had but he dodged me and tripped me.

Falling to the ground I looked at him, "That's cheating, Dad!"

Looking at me with a smile he said, "When your life is on the line there's no cheating. Now, again." The day passed slowly as we trained from sun up to sun down. Father made me throw large rocks telling me it would build strength. He would make me run up and down the small hills until I could no longer move, and then made me fight him. He said that what truly defines a warrior is the breaking point where most would quit, yet a true warrior always pushed past the breaking point and would always be victorious.

We trained day after day for months. Some days, Aleya came and watched us, and sometimes more people. Everyone in town was excited that I was training hard to be a knight. It was amazing to see everyone so happy for what I wanted; they would even bring us food and water at times. The wood workshop would make us swords when we would break the old ones, and they also made us wooden people to practice on.

All I knew was training for those ten long months, and at the beginning of the eleventh month father announced that on the last day of the year he would test me to see if I had passed. Sitting at home in silence I didn't know what to say. We had trained so hard and now he was going to test me in front of everyone.

Walking into the room he sat with me. "Orion, do you know why I told everyone that you had a test coming up?"

Looking away I said, "No."

Patting my head softly he said, "Because you're one of the finest knights I've ever seen, and I want them all to see this too."

His words made me feel so happy. I felt a joy I had never felt, and for some reason I began to cry. As I cried I remembered what I had said to him about mother's death. "Dad, I'm so sorry I said what I did about you not protecting mother. You're amazing, Dad. I know she meant the world to you."

He leaned close and hugged me, "Orion, what you said is true. I should have saved her, and that's why you must become what I could never be."

Pulling back as he held me, he continued to say, "Orion, you must become strong and help as many people as you can. I lived in fear for my entire life and so I was never able to help all the people that I could."

Looking down he held me as he cried. "I'm sorry, my son. I'm sorry I didn't protect your mother." I felt his unbearable pain. I had never seen father cry like this, but I guess he had been hiding his emotions for a long time.

"Dad, I'll become a knight and one day I'll be king."

When I said that I would be king father suddenly stopped, and looked at me. "King? Yes that is what you should be; this land needs a king with a good heart, my son. After your exam we will visit a friend I know in the kingdom, who will surely help us."

Standing up, father smiled at me. "I'm proud of you, my son." Walking into the kitchen he stood staring outside the window, looking at the kingdom. "Orion, the day Stein's walls belong to you, remember where you came from, and help those outside the walls of the kingdom. I believe you'll be king one day, my son, if that's what you truly desire. That is the easy part. However, being king is not as easy as it sounds. One must choose what becomes of the people within your kingdom, meaning the lives of many will be in your hands. Can you handle that?"

Walking closer to father I told him, "I'll have you to help me with that, and I'll always do my best to help everyone."

Turning to me he said, "I know you will, but don't forget helping a person will at times require opposing another, but we'll discuss this more in the future. For now you must focus on being the best knight you can, so people can trust you with their lives and then the rest will come." Father walked me to my room, and as we said our goodnights he walked to his room.

Lying in bed I closed my eyes to rest, but since I was unable to,

I stayed awake thinking about the exams to come and how father believed in me. As I laid there thinking I heard father walking down the stairs, so I stood from my bed and walked to my door. I heard him open the door, and walk outside. *I wonder what he's doing at this time?* Walking down the stairs I saw him talking to a man dressed in black. Moving closer to the window, I faintly heard the man say, "If he's ready, then you may take the vessel." The man handed my father something that I could not see. Suddenly the man looked at me. His eyes were a bright green but he wore a mask with symbols carved into it so I could not see his face. Father then turned towards me, and when he did the man turned away.

I quickly ran up the stairs and into my room. Throwing myself into the bed I closed my eyes and pretended to be asleep. I heard father walking up the stairs. As he stepped into the room I slowly opened one eye to see what he was doing, but he just stood there.

"Orion, go to sleep," he said closing the door.

Father was acting strangely but I laid there thinking of the man's mask. It was strange I had never seen those symbols, and that man's eyes had made me feel uneasy. The more I kept thinking, the more tired I felt, until my eyes finally began to close.

Waking up the next day, I thought that I should get ready for another lesson. Walking downstairs I saw father sitting with breakfast prepared, "Well I know the best way to wake you up is with food, so I made us some breakfast," said father as he finished placing the plates on the table.

As always, he was full of energy. Sitting down we both raced to eat as if we had never eaten in our lives. Once we were done, father stood from his chair and said, "Go and see Aleya. Her mother told me that she'll be leaving soon. I guess her father found a better place to live in the west from what I hear."

Father's news shocked me, so standing up quickly I ran out to Aleya's house. But when I stepped inside she was nowhere to be found and all their belongings were gone. *She left already?* Walking outside I felt sad. I'd been so busy training this past year that we had barely spent any time together.

"Hey Orion, what's wrong?" said a soft voice. Looking up I saw her running towards me. Just looking at her made me feel happy for some reason.

"Aleya, I thought you'd already left?"

Still running towards me she jumped on me and hugged me. "You're sad that I'm leaving?" she said with a smile on her face.

Backing off her I replied with a serious tone. "No, I just have to be kind to women. It's part of the knight code."

She laughed and gave me a kiss on the cheek. "Ok, my knight, or should I say my king, thank you for being so kind, but yes this is my last day here. Father wants us to leave soon. But I'll be back! I wish to study history of the Ashen here in the south, so maybe we'll see each other again."

The news of her leaving made my stomach feel strange, and I didn't know what to say. I felt nervous and sad at the same time. Leaning in closer I kissed her on the lips like I had seen father do when he told mother he loved her. Opening my eyes I saw her eyes wide open as she turned red. Without knowing what to say I walked away. Aleya stood there in silence. Looking back I saw her father and mother talking and telling her to get on the carriage. Aleya stood there looking at me with the same face, until her father made her get inside, but before she did she said, "Thank you for my birthday gift. I'll always remember this day." I watched as she left. "Don't go," I whispered to myself. Had I truly remembered her birthday I would have done something more special for her.

Turning back I noticed my dad standing at the door of our house, "I see you said goodbye to your friend in more than just words. Oh, and son don't worry, she didn't notice that you forgot her birthday. I'm sure that goodbye made her feel really special."

"Yeah, I guess I miss her now," I replied with a nervous feeling.

"Well Orion, when she was here you didn't want her around you, so now you should be a bit nicer with your friends. It's important to cherish the things we have when we have them, not when we lose them," said father as he walked inside.

What he said was true. I had neglected her many times and now that she was gone I wanted her back. Night came and with it no sound, as everyone seemed to stay inside their homes without speaking a word.

Walking outside I climbed onto the roof. As I sat there I started to think about the time when Aleya had asked me why I wanted to be a knight. *She didn't understand me. She said that there was more than one way, but still she wouldn't understand. Her mother wasn't taken from her like mine.*

"Orion, hey what are you doing?" said Leon as he walked close to the house. "I came to apologize. I know I haven't been talking to you lately but, well...I didn't know how to tell you that I liked Aleya, and she, uh...she never talked to me. Look I'm sorry, I hope we can still be friends."

His words made me feel happy, as I missed talking to Leon, "Yeah, it's ok, come up here. It has been a long time since we hung out."

Leon climbed up to the roof and sat next to me, "So I see that you sit here a lot. What do you do up here?"

Looking at Leon I said, "Well I sit here often and think about becoming a knight one day, you know how I told you before."

Looking at the kingdom Leon said, "You still want to do that? I thought you'd given up on those dreams."

Laughing, I insisted, "Leon, I can't give up on those dreams. I'll become a knight one day. Why don't you come with me?"

Leon stood up. "Who knows, maybe one day we can save people together, but I should get going now."

Jumping down Leon said, "Hey Orion, thanks."

"For what?" I asked.

"For being my best friend," he said with a smile.

Walking to his house I saw him smile as if he had released the feelings he had inside. As I walked I felt something odd around me, and peering into the dark forest I spotted a figure hiding behind a tree in the distance.

Afraid, I asked, "Who's there?" Without responding the figure completely hid behind the tree.

I ran inside, scared. "Dad, there was someone looking at me outside. They were hiding behind a tree."

Walking downstairs father came close to me, "Orion, what are you doing outside at this time? It's probably someone just playing with you, son. Now go to bed."

"But dad, it was creepy." Father walked to his room half asleep and closed the door.

Walking to my room, I felt the same presence there, yet looking around I could not find anything. But when I walked over to the window, I saw the same figure walking in the forest, so I ran to my father's room. "Dad, can I sleep in here tonight?"

Laughing he said, "Orion, you're a knight. Knights can't be afraid of the darkness." His words made me feel strong so I walked to my room and held my wooden sword close. "I have to be strong," I said to myself, then lying in bed, I closed my eyes.

The day of the exam came when I'd be named for the knight academy, and everyone in town was excited, making plans for a late night festivity. That same day a man had come to the house and asked father if he would be of help to the kingdom, since a war had broken out between the south and a group of rebels known as the Blood Hand. Father ordered me to leave him and so I left the house feeling a bit upset since he didn't even mention anything about my ceremony. Walking over to the road where the knights always passed, I stood near the path waiting for their return, only to see a handful of men limping, exhausted, injured, with faces of defeat. Yet deep within them I could see strength and honor, and a level of determination that gave me the chills. I stood there watching as each man's face had the expression of loss, for they had lost more than they had gained it seemed, but I could not help but wonder where their strength to continue onward came from.

Walking close to them I noticed one of the men riding his horse without joy nor fear but rather with purpose in his eyes. The man had dark grey hair, with a beard. He seemed a bit older than the rest, yet very strong, as his blue eyes peered at the distance, lost in thought. This man wore heavy armor that covered his entire body except for his right arm, which seemed to be free for his sword. The man noticed me hiding near the brush and paused. The other knights passed him as he stood in place. Turning towards me I noticed him stare right at me.

Afraid of what the knight might say I ran as quickly as possible, moving past the brush. The knight called out my name.

"Orion!" Pausing, in shock as he said my name, I felt my heartbeat hasten. The knight slowly walked towards me and kneeling close he said, "You're that boy who always watches as we come through the gates, are you not?" Nodding my head in agreement, I felt my skin shiver in anxiety.

Leaning in close, the knight placed his hand on my head and said, "One day you'll walk among brave men, and when you do, be more than brave. Be kind, and always keep dreaming as you do, never allowing the defeat of one or a thousand to second-guess your dreams."

Standing up the knight reached into his leather bag, which he carried on his back, pulling out a coin. With a smile on his face he said, "This coin is said to be worth much, but I find little use for it other than a gift for you to always remember this day by." Looking at the coin, I felt true joy as a knight had looked at me as someone worthy of a gift.

Standing up the knight turned around and said, "Your father is proud of you," then rejoining the other knights, he walked away.

Before I left I saw one of the knights in the back wearing all black armor. He was among the last, and something about him made me feel as if he were different. I stood in place waiting for him to pass me by. As he approached, I saw through the knight helmet, bright green eyes; the eyes of a powerful knight. Passing me the knight looked my way, and without a word he continued to move. His horse also had armor and he did not seem to wear the sigils of the south. He carried his enormous sword on his back, unlike the rest who had their swords on their waist.

Stepping back I looked at the sun as it seemed to come down. I had wasted too much time here and I had to run home and get ready for my festival. Making my way back I saw everyone with a smile on their face as the time for me to grow up had come.

*This night will be the night that my dream begins,* I said to myself as I ran inside my house, quickly showering and getting ready.

I was ready within minutes and ran outside. Father was nowhere to be seen, so I stood in front of my house waiting for him. After hours of waiting I saw him at a distance, riding with his horse, wearing what looked like armor. *Father has armor? What does this mean?*

"Hey Orion, come here. Your father said you need to be ready as soon as he gets here. Hurry," said Leon, walking to the middle of the town. I stood as everyone surrounded me. They all looked so happy and I felt overwhelmed, but I knew that this is how it would always be.

Father stepped closer and dismounted the horse. "Orion, kneel." Kneeling down I bowed.

"On this day you're here by committing your life to your people. You'll be their sword and shield. Never forfeiting, never forgetting who you are, you'll always stand for truth and justice. From this day forth you shall seek to graduate as a knight from the Stein academy and become the first to bring unity between those within the kingdom and those outside."

Father touched my shoulder with the sword. "A knight, you shall be," he said as everyone clapped. Father buried the sword in front of me. "Steel is cold, as is war, never forget this." Walking away father mounted his horse, as he rode to the house. Standing up I held the sword as everyone cheered me. I saw father enter our home. Leon walked closer to me and said, "Well, it must be customary to not act soft after you just knighted someone. I guess that's why your dad left like that."

"Yeah," I said, but I knew there was something off. I stayed with everyone as they danced and partied.

After a few hours the party ended and everyone returned to their homes. Leon and I stayed outside, as Leon said, "You know I've never told you but I've been jealous of you my whole life. You always have these big dreams and everyone likes you for it. That made me hate you at first, but for some reason that's why we became friends. I think I wanted to be like you, so I decided to meet you. I don't want to sound bad on the day you graduated but I just wanted to tell you about that, and now more than ever I want you to know that I mean it. I'll be there for you no matter what. I know I'm not as smart as you or as strong as you, but I know that I can do something to help you, Orion." Hugging me he then walked to his house. Looking at me with a smile he said, "Who knows, maybe I'll be the one that gets Aleya."

His words made me smile. I could see that he really did like her, and me, who took her for granted, was the one she liked. I wonder why life makes us stare at the things we want at arm's length. It makes us want things and those things are always out of reach in the end. "Leon, if only you knew that this entire time I've wanted to be like you, to impress you, and now I know that we've both wanted the same. I'm glad we're best friends."

That night I stayed up late looking at the sky with the coin the knight had given me. Realizing he had never mentioned his name I decided to see him first thing in the morning, so I could introduce myself without being afraid. I laid beneath the night sky feeling a sense of joy to think that my name meant something to one of the knights. As I lay still thinking of what to say once I met him again first thing in the morning, I noticed a light in the distance. Looking closer, I soon realized that a group of men wearing armor and carrying swords were slowly creeping closer to the village.

It seemed odd since no one roamed this area at such a late time, so I began to worry as to why these men drew near. Afraid of the uncertainty of their actions, I slowly walked towards my village. Making my way into the village a few of the people waved at me before closing their doors. *Such kind people live with me,* I thought to myself as I continued home.

Opening the door to my house I made my way to my father's room leaning close to him, shaking his arm quickly to wake him up. While moving my father's arm I thought of what the men could do with swords in the middle of the night. My heart suddenly felt a sense of unease as my breathing became heavier with every passing minute.

Startled, my father woke up with an angry look, yelling at me. "What is it, Orion? Why are you up at this time? And why are you waking me up?" His eyes slowly changed as he saw my expression of fear. Leaning closer he whispered to me, "What happened? Why are you so afraid?" With a sense of overwhelming fear I could not speak as my throat felt like it carried rocks.

Slowly whispering to my father, I said, "There are men walking near here with swords, armor, and torches, Dad." My father slowly leaned back as he looked around. Walking close to the door, he picked up his sword. Father always said he'd never use this blade unless it was meant to protect those he loved. At this moment I felt a sense of relief, because father was known to be an exceptional swordsman in our village.

Walking towards me, he leaned close and whispered, "Hide beneath the bed and don't come unless I get you, ok?" I quickly ran under the bed and hid. My mind began to race with thoughts of the unknown events that were about to unfold. Fear quickly made me anxious and restless.

Moments passed and nothing seemed to be happening. There was an utter silence that made me even more afraid, until I heard my father speaking with a group of men. He sounded upset, warning them to leave the village. One of the men laughed as he shouted, "All those who live here belong to the kingdom of the south, and so you're all dogs."

From the fear of his words, my hands began to sweat, and my heart pounded harder. "Dogs, you say? Well maybe this dog should drive you out of here by force," replied my father. Unable to keep my composure, I ran outside the house. My father looked back at me with surprise. "Orion!" he shouted.

The man standing before my father quickly drew his sword. As my father was distracted by my actions, the man pierced the sword through my father's chest. Holding on to the blade as it plunged into him, my father fell back calling out my name in pain. "Orion." The man who stabbed father pushed him to the ground.

"Make sure he doesn't stand back up. I want him to watch this," said the man to his men as he walked closer to me.

Standing there as the men held my father, I watched as they pinned his face to the ground. Tears ran down my face as I screamed for the men to free him. Shouting, I begged for the men to leave my father be, but the more I tried the less the words came out of my mouth as my desperation did not allow me to speak clearly.

Running towards Leon's house, I slammed into the door as if trying to break it. Begging for help, I knocked with desperation, kicking and pounding at the door. But all I could hear was his father telling him to run and hide. I could hear Leon fighting with his father to come out for me, but the father said, "Orion, get away from the door or you'll bring those men this way." Shocked by his words, tears came out of my eyes as I begged him to help me.

Turning back to look around I saw that people were staying in their homes and hiding out of fear. I saw the men laugh at my struggle. The one who had stabbed my father, a tall thin man with blond hair and dark blue eyes came close to me as he said, "See these cowards. Look as they hide from me and my men. Well these are the people you love. Do you see now that no matter who you are or where you are, the one who has power rules over all?"

Placing his blade close to my face the man began to cut it slowly, carving deep into my skin. I felt the cold steel blade slowly open my skin across the bridge of my nose, as its razor sharp edge cut deeper. I saw the man's eyes open wide as if he enjoyed watching me suffer. My eyes were filled with tears and so everything blurred. All I could see was the village, empty and isolated. "Why will no one help me? Why am I so alone? Leon, you said you would be here?"

Petrified by fear I stood still, and time seemed to slow down. The lights from the torches seemed to brighten, as my breathing hastened. I heard my father begging for the man to spare my life, "Please, let my son go. Please, I beg you." My father soon realized the men were unreasonable and so with one last attempt my father gathered enough strength to push the men off him and grab his blade.

Holding his blade with little strength my father rushed towards the man, but because of his wound he moved slowly as he neared the man. Quickly turning to my father the man extended his arm in an instant as his hand caught my father's blade. In that same instant the man quickly thrust his blade, piercing my father's throat.

Laughing the man said, "Silence. Now watch me burn your beloved town to the ground, and take your son from you along with everything you love." Dropping to the floor, as blood poured from my father's mouth, his body began to convulse. Rushing towards him I held his head as he held his throat trying to stop the bleeding as he squirmed for breath.

The wound was deep. Choking on his own blood my father held my hand with a strong grip. Tears ran down his face as he laid there helplessly looking at me. I could feel the warm blood run down my hands, as his lips quivered. My father's hands touched my face as if he were begging me to save him.

The man laughed as he said, "You know now that I think about it, I do remember you. Yes, you're the same man whose wife we took. Oh, she was a pretty one. You were more of a coward back then, as you sat there and watched me and my men have our way with her. You closed your eyes as she squealed like a whore. Now look at you, still a coward, and now you're going to let us have our way with everything you love. How pathetic."

As the man spoke, father opened his hand as I held him, revealing a black crystal. With the crystal he cut my hand and said, "Don't be afraid. This is the king's stone." I could barely see because of my tears but I saw the crystal turn into what looked like black smoke, seeping into my arm. I felt a sudden coldness within me.

A voice within me said, "If death is what you wish then death is what they shall receive; if life is what I should take then that is what I shall do. Release me, give me strength." I didn't know what to feel or what to do as I held my father, but the voice echoed again and again.

With a smile on his face father said, "My king," and releasing all tension his body soon felt lifeless. It seemed unbelievable to think that my father was dead. To think that this man had taken what little I had left from me. Cursing at life itself, while holding my father tightly, I felt my fear slowly burn away. My fear soon turned to rage as my father's lifeless body laid in my hands.

I heard laughter as the men watched from afar and the laughter soon became taunts towards my father's death. I felt disgusted by everyone. Doors from the surrounding houses slowly crept open, merely to see what was happening. But still no one came to help me; no one seemed to care. They were only interested in their own pathetic lives. As I sat there it seemed strange but everything slowly lost meaning and the world around me lost color, everything turning to black and white. The flames turned from red and yellow to a dark black, as fire burned ever brighter. I heard a voice inside my head tell me, "Release yourself, end their lives, and watch them burn and destroy everything, for you are king of kings. Show them true terror, and paint the sky blood red with their bodies."

This voice gave me a sense of welcoming, and it felt overwhelming. I felt alive and powerful. I sensed every person around me and heard their inner voices, which made me sick. In that instant I felt how pathetic humans really are, and how they all deserved to perish. In this moment I heard footsteps as they walked closer to me.

Standing up I turned my face. Looking around me I saw the bodies of all the men scattered across the ground, as their bodies had been torn to pieces. Some men were missing their heads, some their torsos, and others had been cut into shreds. I felt as if this was how it all should be. From afar a black figure walked towards me as it raised its hands to his side to show me what had been done, then pausing at a distance he bowed to me as he faded away. I heard its voice echo, "For you my king."

As the figure faded, I saw Leon for he too had been cut in half. Tears ran down my face, as I screamed, "No Leon, not you, please don't go." My best friend extended his hand towards me. As tears ran down his face he said, "I'm scared." Running towards him I witnessed his eyes close, as he dropped his hand. Gasping for air, I felt confused. What had just happened? Had I done this?" Falling to my side I noticed everything slowly turn back to normal.

Waking up the next day, dazed, I realized the knight with green eyes stood before me as he kneeled down. Taking off his helmet, his long black hair fell down. I saw the pity he felt in the way he looked at me.

"Take this," he said as he handed me some water. "Tell me, what happened here, boy?"

I looked around as the village had been completely burned to the ground, with bodies lying all across the town. "I'm not sure," I lied as the knight turned to face the village and said, "It seems you were targeted by those who we're at war with. They must have seen your village before attacking the kingdom. I'm sorry for your loss, but we should get going as it's not safe here."

"Don't be sorry, I don't care about those people," I said as I stood up.

My words brought a shocking look to the knight's face as he looked at me. Holding my hand he walked me over to a horse as he placed me on the front.

"Tell me boy, have I seen you before?"

"Yes, on the road to the kingdom."

"Is that so? Were your eyes always that green? No other person I know has those eyes besides me."

"My eyes aren't green."

Handing me a dagger he said, "In case you've forgotten, look." Looking at myself with the knife I could see my eyes were indeed a bright green color, and across my face there was a scar that had completely healed.

"I guess I forgot what I look like. Sorry."

"I see, no worries. Let us leave this place. If you wish I can take care of you until we find you a home."

Riding into the kingdom I felt tears slowly trickle down my face. "Did you find the body of a boy close to me?" I asked.

In response he said, "No, why?"

"No reason. I thought someone I knew was close to me in all the chaos. How about a man who looked like me?"

"Yes, was he your father?"

Looking up as we neared the kingdom I said, "He was my mentor."

"It's ok to cry, boy. War isn't easy on the heart," said the knight.

"Orion. My name is Orion, and I'm not crying. I'm going to be a knight and knights don't cry," I said as I tried to hold my tears back.

Patting my head he said, "My name is Nigh, and maybe I can help you get there."

# CHAPTER 2

## BETWEEN FLESH AND STEEL

*The year is 1115*

Time had flashed before my eyes, and over four years had passed since I first came within the walls, but it was all a blur as we woke each day before the sun rose to train, sleeping only when needed. Every breath we took was to train and better ourselves; all that we sought was the discipline and mental sharpness of a true knight. Nigh had taken it upon himself to mentor me, Visan, Adriel, and Anibel. Visan was about my height. We were both smaller than the others, but he was a bit thinner than me, with dark red hair, blue eyes, and pale skin. Adriel was the tallest of us all, standing at almost the same height as Nigh, he had darker skin, brown eyes, and short hair. Anibel was a bit taller than me, with lighter red hair than Visan, deep blue eyes, and pearl white skin with freckles, which people made fun of, yet I thought they were beautiful marks. From the moment Visan and I met, we had barely spoken to one another but Adriel and Anibel had kept us all alive while we trained, since they were always positive.

The first day we were all picked to train under Nigh's watch I remember everyone's face of excitement, since we would train under one of the legendary knights who had made a name for himself in the Blood War, the war against the rebel faction known as the Blood Hand.

Nigh stood before us, silent, observing our every move. Pacing back and forth he said, "Take a seat. Today will be a simple day. I'm interested to know why you're all here. Before I can train any of you I must first evaluate why you wish to march down the field of battle at my side. We'll start with you, Adriel. I hear you're a rather talented swordsman, among the best in your age group from what most say. So tell me what brings you here? Is it because you can swing that sword?"

Adriel smiled. "No Sir. I'm here to serve the south, as all those who are knights do. There's no other reason other than to serve."

Nodding his head Nigh looked at me, "Well, Adriel has shared his answer and honestly I approve, as sometimes the simple dreams are the most rewarding. Now Orion, tell me what brings you here? We've met before but never shared deep words. I hope today you can enlighten me as to why you sit before me."

Taking a deep breath I clinched my fists, feeling nervous, "Well I want to protect the weak, and help those in need. There are many people who aren't as fortunate as those who live within the walls, and so they suffer a great deal. I've lived with those from the outside and they suffer tremendously. Every day is a struggle for life on the outside. Disease, hunger, or even mercenaries claim the lives of many, so maybe one day I can also help those in need."

"You wish to protect the weak, you say? Well that's interesting, because knights play both roles. We're both takers of life and givers of hope, so you may find it rather difficult down the road to hold on to the ideal that you merely protect. But nevertheless, you have my approval; just keep in mind that ideals of such high hopes come at a high price, for with the strength of love comes the hardship of loss."

I knew his words had some truth to them, but still what would he know of the outside, and all we have to endure? I will never give up on the hope to help those in need, whether it is within this kingdom or on the outside walls.

Nigh followed by pointing at Visan, "Now tell me what brings you here? Duty or ideals?"

Visan looked away and said, "Neither, I just wish to be remembered. I wouldn't want to go through this life without being remembered. What I desire most is to obtain strength, a strength that none will ever forget."

"Is that so? You say that being a knight is a display of strength? Well you too may be rudely awakened, for such thoughts that bind you to the brotherhood are illusions. Self-strength doesn't come from a title or the ability to wield a sword, but rather the ability to become more than what life expects of you. A greater purpose than yourself is at the heart of being a knight. Strength is a result of courage and honor, which is where you'll find strength. Luckily, we breathe courage and bleed honor as knights so may you find a path among us. You have my approval, young seeker of strength."

Anibel smiled and stood up, "My turn, right?"

Nigh looked at her, "Yes, now you can share with us why you are here."

Anibel stood with her right hand over her heart, "I'm here to serve and protect the south, to seek honor and aid those in need. I wish to aid my brothers and sisters in arms no matter what the odds, and with my every breath I'll seek justice, no matter what the cost."

Nigh walked closer to Anibel and said, "Justice you say? There's no justice in war, Anibel. We knights spill blood to create peace, creating chaos in the hopes of a better outcome. In the end all we have done is create a vicious cycle without end. If you truly seek justice then try and write a book or give a speech in the hopes to change the minds of men to not wage war in the name of justice. Only then will you find true justice, not here as a knight. What you seek is merely another illusion we have fabricated here to give us the peace we need to sleep at night."

Anibel looked down, as if saddened by Nigh's words.

Nigh looked closer. "Are you sad to hear this truth?"

Anibel looked up again with a smile. "No, not at all, Sir Nigh. I believe that here is where I'll find peace."

Raising his eyebrows in surprise Nigh said, "I approve of you. With such passion I can maybe see justice making its way into the hearts of many, so I will ask one more time. Shall you stay and hope to break the cycle or shall you leave and seek it elsewhere?"

Anibel smiled and said, "I shall stay, Sir."

Nigh nodded his head in agreement and asked us to gather our things. "Such promising students! In my years of service to the crown I've seen men seek many things, from justice to power, even to wealth, but none had the conviction I see in your eyes here."

Adriel asked Nigh with a smile, "Sir. Nigh, may we know what brought you to become a knight?"

Nigh said," In truth I seek to bring hope and balance to this land, but even that is merely an illusion."

After he was done talking I asked, "Do you fight for anything that you can tell us? It sounds like a riddle when you speak."

Turning around he said, "I fight for my men, for those at my side, and I put my life on the line so that they may live to see another day. Nothing less, nothing more."

His answer was simple. He fought merely to protect those he cared for. That may be enough for him but not for me. How could any man settle for that? But even then I felt as if there was more to be said.

Looking back at us he said, "Make sure you all take some time to rest, as later this night you will come with me. We'll sleep on the outside of the kingdom. This way we can all take a moment away from this structure and dedicate some time to thoughts. You see, many have grown far too comfortable living in the confinements of their walls, never leaving their homes unless necessary. One thing I've learned during these many years is that the wild gives us an inner awareness of self that we have lost. Isn't that right, Orion?

"Yes, Sir Nigh."

Nigh said, "I won't keep you all from attending to your needs before the sun sets, so make sure you bring water and something for the cold. See you here when the sun sets."

We all walked our separate ways. While Nigh sat in place, he seemed lost in thought, so I decided to walk back towards him. "Sir Nigh, may I have a word with you?"

Without looking at me he said, "Sure Orion, what is it?"

"Well I don't know, but you always look like you're thinking about something. I'm sure it's none of my business but may I ask what always has you thinking?"

"No need to think that it is none of your business, Orion. I have no need to hide anything, but I suppose I lose myself in the past. There's something both soothing and terrible when one digs deep within the mind. Earlier you asked me what I fight for. I seldom answer such a question with detail, but in truth, Orion, every man fights for something few ever realize. I've seen men divide themselves because of faith, because of kingdoms, or because of the color of their skin. You see, we manage to create barriers between one another for no true reason other than fear. Tell me, Orion, when you think of your past, what comes to mind? May I know?"

Looking away I realized what he had just asked me is what I had asked, and despite the oath of being open I felt a sudden hesitation to tell him the truth. "I see. I'd never thought of it as such, but I can see the division all through the lands. As for me, I can only think about the days I trained with my father, and my friends. Those were times that I will never forget. That's all that really comes to mind. I mean, right now it's all I can think of."

Nigh stood up, "Is that so? You know, someone once told me that this world is filled with strange things, some that we could never imagine to be real. Astreya said that there was no need for superhuman abilities in order to have an edge in the outcome of events. This woman was one of the rare few who could best me with a sword. She was as swift as air and as deadly as fire. But what gave her the edge in battle wasn't just her swordsman skills, but rather what she called the power of observation. After training under her mentorship I was able to see what she could see. The world became clear to me. You see people, by nature, lie and they seek to gain the upper hand at any given chance. Fearing exposure, they all hide behind walls of lies. Just now, you lied to me, possibly because your past is one you wish not to share with others, or maybe you have shame in its truth. Regardless of the case, I don't question why you must lie, but when you do, never look to your left; those are the eyes of one who constructs an image in his mind to deceive others. In other words people look to the left before they lie, just as you did now before responding. The one who trained me taught me this. How she knew this is beyond me, however it has never failed me. Am I right?"

Nigh left me feeling stunned. He was able to see through so much in such little time, I could not help but be truthful. "Yes, I'm sorry Sir Nigh. I know it violates the code of the knight. I swear it won't happen again."

Nigh smiled as he walked away, "Orion, you shall lie to me again and to many more. You see, the code of knights is the true virtue of laws to live by. However, they go against our nature, as we humans aren't so honorable at heart; we just desire the construct of it. Make sure you weigh your options before you make the decision to lie, for some may be so great that they would tarnish all that you are. Never forget that in this world the name we bear carries with it all your actions beyond death, so take care to be a man who makes it his honest desire to always reach out to the honor of knighthood."

"I'll always do my best to keep true to what we learn and your words, Sir Nigh."

"Now if there's nothing else to speak of, you should go and ready yourself for the night."

"Yes, if you'll excuse me."

I quickly turned around and walked towards my chambers. Oddly enough, Nigh had managed to not only keep his thoughts out of the conversation but he had managed to make me second guess ever asking him anything personal again. Now I could see why he was revered as a living legend by many. Not only was he skilled with a sword but he was also able to see through people.

Finally reaching my room I noticed a knight walking at the end of the hallway, who seemed very familiar. Thinking to myself, I soon realized that it was the same knight I had met on the road, the one who had given me the coin. It had been so long and I had never seen him again, so without hesitation I ran towards him.

"Excuse me, Sir!" I said loudly.

Looking back towards me, I saw his face, and it was indeed the same man. "Yes, how may I help you, young one?"

"Well, we met a while back on the road, and you gave me this coin." Showing him the coin I saw him smile.

"Well, it seems age is taking its toll on me. How are you, little one? It has been some time. I heard what happened. I'm sorry for your loss."

Nodding my head I said, "Yeah, I'd rather not talk about that." I felt my stomach get heavy as it seemed everything kept bringing my past back.

"Sorry, but you're right. It's best to move forward. Now, tell me what have you been doing all this time? I see you've grown quite a bit, and now it seems you're letting your hair grow and are using the same hair style as Nigh."

"Well I've been training to become a knight. Nigh is my mentor, and he has been dedicating time to our training."

"Nigh? Now that makes you lucky. He's one of the most admirable men with a sword I've ever seen. Well after me that is," he laughed.

"Really?

"We'll just keep that between you and me. Now tell me, you said it is you and others?"

"Yes it's me, Visan, Adriel, and Anibel. We're all from the same squad."

"I see, well you're all in good hands. Now before I leave tell me what your name is again? It slips my mind."

"Orion, and that reminds me, what's your name? You never told me when we met."

"Oberon. Now we've formally met, who knows, maybe I'll teach you something sometime. Do me a favor and tell Nigh I've finally made my way back to the kingdom from the tower of Elysium in Alluvium. Tell him to come and see me when he's able to, as I have some news he might want to hear. Now you take care and make us all proud, young Orion."

Sir Oberon walked away. Seeing him again made me feel joy. He wasn't like Nigh who was always lost in thought, but rather he seemed to always smile."

Making my way to my room, I quickly gathered my things, and looking outside the window I saw the sun set. Staring at the red sky I thought about the many days I had spent on the roof of my house, always imagining myself as a knight, and on this day I was one step closer to joining the knights. But for some reason I could not smile. All I could see was my village burn. *Why can't I just forget that night?* I thought to myself as I closed my eyes.

Closing my eyes, I felt a sudden warmth, as if something had surrounded me with a burning flame. I found myself standing in the middle of my village, where darkness consumed it. Standing in place I witnessed it all burn: the people, the homes, the trees, and in the midst of the flames my friend, Leon, was on his knees. As he cried out, I walked closer to him, and standing in front of him I could hear him, "No matter what, I'll always be at your side." Looking to my right a hand, made from black smoke, reached out, carving a symbol in the shape of a star on his head. Suddenly I awoke startled, with Anibel standing above me.

"Orion, are you ok? I found you on the floor. You were shaking, and your eyes looked white."

"What? I guess I was sleeping. I was just standing here and then I had a dream. But I feel fine, I'm sorry."

"Eww, you dream like that? I feel sorry for your wife. Well I suppose mother always said I shouldn't judge people, so let's go. I think we may be late."

"Wait, what's that supposed to mean?" I asked angrily.

"Nothing," she said, laughing.

Looking outside I could see the sun had already set. "What time is it?"

"I'm not sure as I never look at the time. It makes me worry and I like to stay calm," she said with a smile.

Anibel always smiled and had a rather strange way of thinking. Maybe I could never compare her to Aleya, but she was amazing in her own strange way. Thinking to myself I still pictured the image of Leon's face. It all seemed so real. I couldn't believe that I had such a terrible dream. But why did it all feel so real, as if it were a memory and not a dream?

"Let's go," I told her, as we ran down the stairs and back to where we were supposed to meet Nigh later.

Standing with his arms crossed, Nigh looked at us with anger. Visan and Adriel shouted, "You two are late."

Nigh followed with, "Tonight you'll sleep without a tent, so I hope you brought something to keep you warm."

Turning around they walked forward, while we followed. Visan looked back at me with a smirk. Adriel looked at Visan, "Hey don't laugh, they may have had a reason."

Looking back Nigh said, "Yes, and as a team I think you should all find out what that reason was by joining them on the outside."

Everyone looked at me with a rather upset face. I felt horrible for having placed them in this situation. We continued to walk forward, passing the gate, and entering the forest that surrounded the kingdom. Not too far ahead I saw a fire, with the area clear of leaves and stones surrounding the fire to keep it contained. It seemed it had been preset. I can imagine Nigh had been out here preparing this for us. Despite his cold attitude towards us I knew he cared for us.

Reaching the campfire, Nigh stood in the middle. Looking up at the sky he said, "Take a seat. We should take some time to relax now." Taking a seat we all stayed quiet while Nigh gathered some wood. Walking towards the fire he tossed the wood inside. "This should keep it going for a little while," he said. Thinking to myself as I looked at the others, I observed them all as they were all so different, each with a different life and reason for being here.

Visan, the son of a merchant grew up in a family of wealth, but when his father passed away he became homeless, since his mother left the kingdom for unknown reasons. It seemed this had made him a rather closed person. Despite all my attempts to strike a conversation with him, he refused to make any effort to talk, making it hard to understand him.

Adriel is one of the most talented swordsmen I've ever seen; he's just a year older than me and has managed to pass every test flawlessly. Always with a smile on his face I can see that he hides something deep within. No one has asked where his parents are but we all know that he keeps his personal life to himself. We have quickly become good friends. In a way he reminds me of Leon so maybe that's why I've been able to openly sit and talk with him about my dreams of becoming a knight.

Anibel has the most cheerful personality I've ever seen in anyone. Her parents are the same. They're all people of good hearts. After having lost Aleya, I managed to put my feelings of solitude aside and have made sure to dedicate time to her and the others. Sometimes I sit with her and think to myself, if maybe I'd have spent more time with Aleya, would she have stayed? But after everything that happened, her leaving was for the best. Anibel always brings Aleya to mind, and so I tend to spend more time with her than anyone. I feel selfish knowing I spend time with her merely to remind myself of another friend, but it makes me feel the comfort I once felt with Aleya.

The night had become rather cold and foggy, so we all gathered around closer, placing our hands near the flames. Staring into the flames I watched the bright fire burn the wood. While the wood crackled everyone's voice around me faded, and Visan and Anibel were talking about how cold it was, but I could barely hear their voices. Time seemed to slow down. As I stood up I saw the flames of the bonfire turn black and follow me, wrapping themselves around me. I felt the warmth of fire upon my skin but it did not hurt, rather it felt soothing. They all sat in silence, no one moved so much as an inch. The flames from around me reached out slowly towards everyone, burning through them. I saw all of their skin slowly turn to ashes, except Nigh. As the flames circled him they could not reach him. Looking around I was speechless. Was this another dream or was this reality?

The world slowly turned a grey color, as the pitch black flames quickly burned through the forest. Closing in on the kingdom I turned to look as everything was set aflame, and the walls of the kingdom fell. The wooden homes fell apart, while people screamed in agony as smoke covered the sky. Looking back smoke slowly covered Nigh's body, as he kneeled with his sword piercing the ground. He looked upon me as the ashes slowly touched his face. Everything around him turned completely into ashes, and scattered into the wind as his hair turned a white color and his skin peeled revealing a pale silver, while his eyes were slowly covered inside turning them completely black. Walking closer to Nigh something made me want to reach out to him, and as I did my hand slowly turned to ashes. Suddenly I found myself once again in complete darkness. I had been here before, and it all felt too familiar, but what was the meaning of this?

This place must be real. I knew that I could not just keep imagining this over and over again. It felt as if there was someone here with me, trying to reach out to me. The darkness slowly turned grey, and I found myself in an old throne where everything seemed to be made of iron and stone, as fire covered the area. "This place, I've been here before," I whispered to myself. Walking forward I saw a young boy sitting on the throne, reading a book. While holding the book his eyes turned a bright red color, as he smiled with a sinister smile.

The boy looked up at me. "I've been waiting, young vessel."

His words echoed and as he spoke everything went dark. Once again I found myself back at the camp near the bonfire, with everyone else. Visan and the rest were still talking about being cold as if nothing had happened.

Looking around I stood up. "Sir Nigh, may I have a moment? I want to take a walk."

Nigh nodded his head. "Yes, just be careful."

Walking into the woods, I could not believe how real it all seemed. The fire, the ashes, the kingdom burning, that boy sitting reading that book. I had no idea what it meant, so I walked closer to a stone and decided to sit down. I knew there was something trying to reach out to me, so I decided to seek it out myself.

Sitting on the stone I closed my eyes, "I am here, what do you want?" I said with anger. The wind picked up around me, opening my eyes. I leaned back startled, as a figure within a cloud of dark smoke stood before me. All I could see was the faint image of what looked like a knight, as it stared at me, extending its hand towards me.

This was the same figure I kept seeing, so it was true this was not a dream. Getting closer I reached out with my hand, but then I heard Nigh call out my name. The figure turned its head towards where the sound came from, vanishing. Quickly closing my eyes again I tried to once again call for it, but nothing showed, so I tried again and again but still nothing appeared.

Making my way to the camp I saw Nigh putting out the flames. "Orion, get some rest. Tomorrow we'll make our way around the area to meet with some old friends of mine for some classes."

"Yes, Sir Nigh," I said with a rather aggravated voice, as he had interrupted me reaching out to whatever it was that had tried to call for me.

Laying in the darkness thoughts crossed my mind. *Why do I not feel fear towards this? What is this internal urge to seek for whatever this thing is? And why do I feel the need to keep it to myself? A part of me feels as if there's another side of me fighting against me. It's a strange feeling, but I know that I can't tell anyone about this, or they may think I have gone mad.*

The following day we all gathered our things and made our way deeper into the forest. As we walked I soon realized that I had never told Nigh that Oberon had asked for him to see him. "Sir Nigh, I apologize but there was a knight who wished to speak with you. Oberon he said was his name, but I forgot to tell you."

Nigh looked at me with an angry face. "You forgot? Orion, those things can be rather important, you know. Now tell me, did he say why he wanted to see me?"

"Sorry, Sir Nigh, he didn't say."

"Okay, well it's good to know he's ok. The rest of you go on ahead. Just around that cliff are Vivian, Straif, and Zangar. Introduce yourselves and let them know I'll be there soon. I have to have a word with Orion first."

They all agreed and continued to walk. I was afraid that Nigh was upset with me and that's why he wanted to have a word with me. Nigh walked close to a log and sat down. "Orion, come sit, we need to talk." Walking over I sat next to him, and I could feel my palms sweat with a strong feeling of anxiety as he stared at me.

"Orion, the reason I asked you to stay here with me is because from the day I met you I've seen you always with this look in your eyes as if you're chasing something. Tell me, what is it that has you like this? The others are worried; I can see it in their faces, especially Anibel. Last night, while we sat around the fire, you seemed lost again, but more so than most times. I told you that I observe everything, and something about this has me thinking of what lingers in your mind. The day I found you in your village, I could see the light from your eyes had completely faded, and from that day I've never seen it come back. What I'm trying to say is that you've lived through enough. Maybe you should think about turning down knighthood, as it will only get worse."

Nigh's words made me feel anger, as I heard the pity he had for me. "Sir Nigh, you also spend most of your time lost in thought."

"Yes, this is true, but I'm a man with a past, Orion. You're merely a boy, so there's no reason for you to have the eyes of the lost, as we call it."

"The lost? What do you mean?"

"The lost are the knights who have lost their faith, their light, and their soul in the battlefield. These are men who have seen the horrors of war many times, and may still live in flesh but are dead in spirit."

I knew Nigh wanted me to quit here but I refused. "I won't quit. I admit I've been sad because of what happened before you found me but I've not lost myself. I know it's something I can't forget, but that's the reason I can't quit. If I quit then all their lives would have been lost in vain. I made a promise to my father, and to my friend, Leon. I will become a knight, and I will protect the weak, and help others. I can't just sit and watch all the bad keep growing in the world."

Nigh placed his hand on my shoulder. "Are you sure? If you leave now no one will blame you."

Looking at the sky as father often would, I said, "Yes, I'm sure. There's no life for me outside of knighthood." While staring at the sky I saw father smile.

"I see. I admire your determination, however I hope you realize that you won't change the world without it changing you as well. We all have a past. This is the truth, and fortunately for you I've seen potential in you. As of today, you'll be my pupil, and I your master. Consider yourself fortunate. I'll teach you how to make their bodies your strength, and with this you'll be unmatched, but never forget what I'll teach you can only give strength to someone who seeks to help others, for that's where the heart of knighthood lays.

*What Nigh said may be true. There may be much risk in what I desire but if I run in fear and hide like most, then how could I ever hope to see peace in this world?* "Sir Nigh, thank you. I'm honored to have you as my master," I responded with gratitude, but a part of me still was in disbelief, as it seemed he had this in mind all along.

Nigh walked away. "Let's go then. We'll join the others and see what the result of their meeting was."

We both made our way to where the others had gone. Getting closer I heard Visan speaking with someone who had a deep voice. Around the corner I noticed a woman and two men. One was large and full of muscle. A rather impressive sight, his tanned skin was filled with scars and his hair was long and red, with a beard to compliment it. The other man was smaller, and stood with a robe and a pole weapon made of wood. Beneath the robes I saw armor. His left hand had leather gauntlets and his right hand actual armor. With long black hair and skin pale white he stood out. His right eye was scarred, only having his left eye open. The woman wore a long blue dress, and around her face she wore a silk cloth. All that I could see were her red lips faintly behind the cloth, and her brown eyes, that stood out with her pale skin.

Nigh walked ahead of me. "Well, it seems we've all come together then. Vivian, Zangar, Straif, meet Orion, my new pupil."

The large man walked closer to me, "Hey little one, nice to meet you. I'm Zangar, one of your master's mentors."

"Hello, Sir Zangar."

Zangar looked at Nigh and spoke, "Hey Nigh, this one is rather small. Have you fed him?"

Nigh smiled, "Yes, he's still young, Zangar."

The woman stood in place, "I'm Vivian. Nice to meet you."

Vivian's eyes stared at me and made me feel shy. Her beauty and the soft tone of her voice would make any man feel the sudden warmth that comes with a presence of a lovely woman.

The other one sighed. "Enough of this. We must begin training, I'm sure you can deduce who I am."

Zangar turned around and said, "You're so arrogant. It might be because of that crazy master of yours."

The man turned around, "My name is Straif. Come now Anibel, we must go. They plan on wasting time here."

Anibel seemed afraid, but she knew she had no choice; she had to go with her new master. Zangar walked towards Visan. "Well, we should head back. Now that I recall the king wants to know the details of the training. But before I leave I'll tell you all that you have proven yourselves as the top students and thus you'll be the leaders of the four squads. I'm sure Straif will let Anibel know of this. We'll see you soon. Let's go little Visan."

Walking away, they too left, as Vivian walked behind them. "Follow me Adriel, we'll go with them." Pausing for a second she looked back. "Coming Nigh?"

Nigh scratched his head. "It's best if I stay behind. I have things to discuss with Orion. Can you please tell the king that we'll be there tomorrow? He still has some training to do."

Vivian turned around, "Sure, just don't kill the kid."

"I won't, Vivian. I'll see you soon."

Her last words made me step back wondering why we were going to stay out here for another night. Nigh turned to me, "I wish for us to talk, Orion. There's much for us to discuss. Before we begin this training there are things you and I must talk about."

Nodding my head in agreement, I walked towards a log and sat down. Nigh walked to where I was sitting and pulled out his sword. "You see this? This is an instrument of death, fear, peace, and revenge. There are endless truths to the sword, but some swords bear with them something beyond what we humans understand. The reason I wish for you to stay here is to explain to you what few know. You see, many years ago, across the narrow seas, in a forgotten land, man sought guidance, and in this time of uncertainty rose a man many would say was the son of the creator. This man would be the first king, and he would go on to build the most beautiful kingdom ever imagined. The king married a woman far from their lands, said to have golden eyes, and pitch black hair. Soon after, they would have two sons, born on the same day. The boys would grow to one day build their own kingdoms. However, jealousy and greed brought the boys to wage war with one another. In his grief for their hatred towards one another the father banished them both from the lands. They would be sent to the far distant land where the mother had come from, as legend has it they were brought here to our very lands. These lands were unknown to them and without kingship, there was no guidance. Here they would go on to build the kingdoms as we know them. The north was the last of the kingdoms to be built, and from the north years later one of the brothers had two boys who would go on to travel back to the forgotten land, only to find it in ruin. From the two brothers only one made it back to these lands, and he was said to have been changed into a beast. Calling himself the Father of Alchemy, he spoke of seeing the throne of the creator, and that it stood empty. The man said that all that was found was what he called the Codex. The Father of Alchemy returned to the north wishing to see his father. Upon seeing the now transformed beast, the king of the north ordered his execution, but after countless attempts to kill the Father of Alchemy, it was evident that he could not die. His father banished him from the north, stating that he was no son of his, just a beast. Using the Codex the Father of Alchemy would go on to bestowing weapons of great power upon those who were deemed fit to rule in his eyes or maybe to see man wage war with one another. After all he had lost everything and would now have to live for all eternity bearing witness to the cruel nature of man. However, in time the artifacts were lost, the weapons were few and far between, and the Father of Alchemy was never heard of again, until the Ashen war, where many of his crafted weapons and artifacts were destroyed by the golden knight, known as the hero of the Ashen war. The golden knight would both disappear with the Father of Alchemy amidst the war and chaos. This sword I hold here is Cinder, one of the few remaining weapons given to man by a being beyond our understanding. Each weapon was hand crafted by the Father of Alchemy, and each wielded the power of thousands. Cinder is said to consume the life force of its wielder in order to conjure the flames of the depths."

I sat there feeling confused about what Nigh was saying. "Sir Nigh, I'm confused. Why are you telling me this?"

Sitting next to me, Nigh said, "Orion, the sword of fire warms to the presence of you for some reason. This has only happened one other time in my life, and now it has happened again with you. The truth is that I've chosen you as my pupil because I believe there's something great within you. Who knows, maybe one day you'll be a leader of men, a man who helps many to live a better life, as you say."

Nigh's words brought a smile to my face. "You think so? How can you tell? Merely because your sword reacts to me?"

Standing up Nigh presented the sword to me. "Here, grab it."

"Are you sure?" I hesitated.

"Yes."

Reaching over to grab the sword, I felt an enormous heat come from it. Wrapping my fingers around it, I felt a sudden surge of energy run through my body. Suddenly the sword lit up with intense heat, as the flames turned black. Nigh grabbed the sword from my hands as the flames vanished.

"I'm sorry, I didn't mean to," I said.

"No need to be sorry. It's just as I thought. You're no ordinary boy, and I know this, but I've never seen the flames of the sword turn black so quickly. I myself have reached this point only once before in my past. The presence was rather strange. I've never felt a flame so intense."

Extending his hand with the sword, fire once again ignited from the sword, but with even more power than mine, the flames turned a dark purple color. "And that's just the beginning. Wait until you see what this sword can really do," Nigh smiled.

Putting his hand down, he said, "Few know of this, and most who see it don't live to tell about it, but I only use this to protect what I care for. Since you're now my pupil, I wanted you to see this. Luckily you weren't afraid of this at all, as if you are familiar with such things. Which brings me to yet another question. Orion, what have you seen? Is there something you're keeping from me? I have a feeling that you're holding something from me."

Now I understood. Nigh suspected me of having something that I was hiding and that's why he had brought the subject of the primordial's, and his sword. "No, there's nothing I'm hiding, master." Any regular person would have freaked out from seeing a sword light up in flames the way his sword did, but I stood there as if it were normal to see such a thing.

"Once again, you lie to me. You see, that split second you hesitated to answer because you were weighing your options and analyzing the situation. Orion, you're dismissed. I'm highly disappointed that you have such little trust in me. I shall not ask anymore, but just know that I shall not be able to train one who does not devote himself to me."

Nigh had placed a lot of pressure on me. I knew then that if I didn't tell him something to satisfy his need to know, he wouldn't train me and possibly disband me from the knight academy. But if I didn't tell him the truth, he would know, and that time I didn't move my eyes, so he was obviously able to sense people's lies in many ways. "Master, yes there's something I've seen. I've had dreams of a shadow that kills people, but I don't know what it is. I'm sure it's just a dream but it feels so real, and sometimes I feel like it wants to talk to me."

Nigh squinted his eyes, "You speak the truth, Orion. Tell me, have you told anyone of this?"

"No, none know, Master."

"Good. Keep this to yourself, not even the king may know. You see, this land has a dark history, and in the past there were stories of things many didn't understand and this brought about great chaos. Like I said, few know of my sword, but it's merely a relic of old, so it bears no ill feeling in anyone's heart. However, what you speak of sounds of demonic origin. It may be a holy blessing, but most will not see it as such, for humans fear what they do not understand."

I looked at Nigh. "I promise I won't tell anyone."

"Well, then let's leave this subject alone for now. I'm sure you've had enough for one day. Maybe we, too, should head back, as that way you can rest in your quarters."

I agreed and we quickly walked back to the kingdom. Nigh parted ways with me at the gate and headed to see Oberon, while I walked straight to my room. Throwing myself in bed I closed my eyes and thought to myself, *What's going on here? Nigh seems to know so much, but how? And now he knows what I can see, but I must not tell him too much. I wish whatever it is could just show itself and tell me what it wants.*

Closing my eyes I felt my body slowly slip into the exhaustion of these long days. I knew that Nigh was a good man, and for some reason I knew he was someone I could trust. He was the one who had rescued me from the ashes of my burned village, after all.

Waking up the next day I began my training with Nigh, and from the moment I opened my eyes until the moment I fell asleep, Nigh pushed me to my limits. Replacing my meals with small portions, he also demanded I always carry my sword to build my strength and bond with my sword. Making me sleep in the cold and sometimes having me only eat what I could catch, he trained me to survive. Every day we carried our swords, we fought with our swords, we cleaned our swords, and we slept with our swords. "The life of a knight is only complete when he and his sword become one," said Nigh.

Nigh had forbidden me to look at the time while I was in training with him, but I always counted the sunrise and the sunset. There had been 460 sunrises since the day we started to train, and every moment of it felt as if all I ever knew was fading. My body had become numb, my mind sharp, and my senses that of an animal hunting by night and training by day. The moments in between I would rest my body but never my mind, for it was always on alert. Nigh would ambush me with success at first but over time I would know his coming well before. After six hundred suns, my training had finished. Nigh stood before me with his blade in hand and granted me with his second blade. Once a sword of great power, he said, but now a rather short blade that had been broken centuries ago.

"Orion, I once stood before you, as you lay in the ashes of the fallen, defeated and lifeless, yet here I see a boy who has become a man. The once frail hands who wielded wooden swords now have taken upon them the cold steel, along with your mind and body, which have also matured a great deal. You may not have noticed but you have outgrown what clothes you had, and one can see the hard work which you have endured. Today you've graduated my training, and to show proof of this I wish for you to take Glave, a memento of a long past war."

Taking the sword I fell to my knees with joy because I'd finally completed the training. Close to finishing the year, I'd now be given some time to rest before it was time to seek the king's approval. Everyone else had trained with their mentors and would graduate on this day also. As for those who hadn't been assigned masters they had finished their training a bit earlier, but from what I'd heard they had all received excellent training under the supervision of Oberon, Alkire, and Zol, said to be at the top of the ranks in terms of skill. They took upon the tasks of training the masses because of their long standing with the knights. They had retired from the grueling training involved with being masters.

Finally the time had come. We had all made it with the exception of few who had quit, and one who had died while training, an incident of rare occurrence but not impossible since we trained with real swords during the second half of the course. But now was not the time to grieve since I had just stepped towards the line of becoming a knight. Now was my time to shine in the light of knighthood and stand at the side of my master, Nigh, to march with him into battle.

"Master Nigh, thank you. I've dreamed about this moment all my life."

"Orion, believe me, there's much to come. Do not thank me just yet. First wait and see if this is truly what you have desired all these years. In truth, we never know what we desire until the moment it has come and gone from our lives."

"Master, no matter what may come, this is all I've ever dreamed of, and nothing will change that."

"We shall see."

# CHAPTER 3

## WITHIN THE VISIONS

*The year is 1117*

The hour was late. I lay in bed, in the darkness of my room, as the shadows of the trees slowly danced around with the passing wind; shadows brought to life by the radiant light of the moon, a moon that showed itself completely tonight. Looking outside my window at the dark of the night, I thought of those who I would never see again. I felt the desolation and devastation of everything that had long since left my side. I spent each night thinking of Aleya, what had become of her life, and where she was now. The sight of their bodies scattered through the burning village never faded from my mind, but even more so the feelings of hatred. Still, there were many parts of that night unclear to me. I did not know if they were dreams or reality. It had been years since the night everything I held dear was taken from me. I was unable to even share warm words with my father. The thought of him dying in my arms still made me feel this empty anger within. To think people were capable of such cruelty. They massacred my entire village and they did so with a smile. But I always wondered how I survived, how I was able to live past that night.

As the thoughts faded from my mind I began to shiver with the cold of the night creeping through the open window. "The night is cold. If only I could find warmth within these walls. Why have windows that can't be closed?" I whispered to myself as I turned my face to an empty room, a room fitting for someone without status. All that could be seen was a door, shelves for the books I wish I owned, and a set of drawers. But even as empty as this room was, it was part of the dream that I had dreamed of my entire life.

"Orion, are you awake?" said a soft voice.

"Yes, but I'm about to rest. Who is it?"

"It's Aleya," whispered the voice.

Walking towards the door, I opened it, only to find that there was nothing to be seen, just an empty hallway. Once again I had heard the voice of someone from my past. Every night I dreamed of those who I had lived with, and every night I questioned myself. I questioned why I had felt so much hate back then for them and why I mourned them so much now.

After hearing Aleya's voice I decided to walk to the top of the kingdom so that I could take some time to think to myself. Making my way to the stairs I noticed the shadows swiftly move around as the long white curtains from the enormous windows flapped with the gusting wind.

"The night seems so alive. The walls seem to have come to life, as the shadows from the curtains slowly move. I can feel as if something calls to me. I can feel that something seeks me, something calls to me."

Walking past the curtains I noticed, in the distance, the shadow made of black smoke at the end behind the final curtain, standing still as it raised its hand towards me. Walking forward to reach out to it I said, "You have waited a long time to show yourself again. What are you?" But when I asked it slowly faded as if made of smoke. I continued to walk forward to see if it still lingered nearby when suddenly I heard a deep voice.

"What brings you here at this hour, young man?"

Looking back I saw a man of pale complexion, and long black hair with crimson colored eyes, wearing black robes.

"I'm sorry, I had to get some fresh air," I said as I walked back past the man.

"You seem afraid of something. Tell me what has you so afraid?" asked the man with a suspicious tone.

"Nothing Sir, I'm just a bit tired."

"Is that so? Well do you mind joining me for some fresh air? I seem to not be able to sleep well these nights. It seems you're unable to sleep too, so maybe good conversation can allow us both to ease our restless minds."

"Uh sure," I complied, as he walked in front of me.

Laughing, the man said, "Well I'm glad some of us don't sleep well. It gives me some company. By the way, what did you say your name was? I don't believe I've ever met you."

"My name is Orion. I arrived here two years ago."

"Oh I see. You're that boy Nigh told me about, the one from the outside village. My condolences to your family and friends. I hear you're quite the brave knight these days. Nigh speaks very highly of you. He's a rather reserved knight but nevertheless one who shines as a true knight, so to hear him have great admiration for his student truly shows that you have a rare trait."

"Thank you. I still haven't made it past the king's approval, so I'm not a knight yet, but I hope to get there soon. So, who are you? Sorry to ask. I just wish to know what name to call you, Sir?"

"No worries, Orion. My name is Sir. Logan, and I am in charge of alchemy. It is a rather dull subject to many so I'm sure you haven't heard of me before. I'm not as famous as Nigh, who's the leader of the Abyss Knights, but rather a man devoted to the science of medicine, the art of life, and the secrets it holds."

"The art of life and its secrets? That sounds interesting. I believe I've heard Sir. Nigh mention your name in the past, but I'm not too sure of what alchemy is. I believe that a friend said her father was an Alchemist Doctor."

"Is that so? Well there are few alchemists these days. The art of science is not one many approve of, as they say we seek to mimic the creator's power. Tell me, what was the name of this friend of yours?"

"Her name was Aleya. She moved from the east to my village when we were children. Her father was a doctor, but he had an accident and was unable to sustain his job in the east so they moved to the south to find a new life. Unfortunately it didn't go so well for them, but the last I heard they found a good life near Minaria to the west, since they were lucky enough to have left the village before it was attacked."

"Aleya? The name sounds familiar. I knew a man by the name of Albert who had a daughter named Aleya. I'm sure we do not speak of the same man, for he was no doctor, but rather a thug, a thief, and an imposter."

Thinking to myself I remembered Aleya's mother calling to her father by the name of Albert. "Are you certain, Sir. Logan, because they do have the same name? My friend's father's name was Albert."

"I see. Well I hope we don't speak of the same person."

"I hope we don't either, since the man you speak of was a bad person."

"Not just that, but because that man was killed recently, hung for treason, and his daughter was sold as a slave."

Logan's words crushed my soul. "How do you know? And when did this happen? Why would she be sold as a slave when her mother would still be alive?"

"Orion, calm down. We don't know if this is your friend. Be more hopeful, and well, I'm always aware of the affairs of other kingdoms. It's part of my duties. I had been tracking Albert for some time because he was a pretender, and one who would have tainted the name of alchemy more than it already is, something I wouldn't allow."

With anger I tried to calm myself down. "I agree, I won't take this to heart. I'll try to focus on what I'm sure of and becoming a knight, for that's what matters most at the moment. Hopefully one day I can hear of her, just to know she's safe."

"Don't try and do anything rash. Your graduation is coming soon, Orion, but also do not forget those precious to you. You will find few in this life are worthy of such a place in your heart."

Thoughts had come to mind to try and reach Minaria so that I could see Aleya myself; a crazy thought but the urge was present. Clearing my mind of the thoughts I said, "No worries, Sir. Logan. I don't intend to do anything rash."

Sir. Logan paused. "Sometimes the hard truth can lead to better outcomes. I'm certain it pains you to even think your friend was sold into slavery, but all men shall feel pain in this life, Orion, and before the time comes for you to take your last breath, you shall love, mourn, and feel things you never imagined. The reason I tell you this is so that you ready yourself for a new world. Once you become a knight the world as you know it shall change forever. No longer will you see kingdoms the same. No longer shall a sun rise and set as it should. No day shall be merely another day in your life. Each day shall weigh heavy on your thoughts. Each moment will impact others lives, and everything you do will either save a life or take a life. This is what you will have to burden."

"You're right. I know that this is something I shouldn't concern myself with. I know my problems are trivial in comparison with everything I'll have to endure."

"No, I don't wish for you to think of it as such. One man shall look upon another man's pain and sympathize with it, but it doesn't mean he understands it. Every person burdens themselves with what they hold precious to their lives. What I'm telling you is to not crumble at the mere sight of loss, of pain, and the hardships of life. Be strong, Orion. The days to come shall test your will, and when you least expect it, life shall turn all that you know into dust, a quickly fading sight of what once laid before you, will be gone forever, in the ever changing sight of life. A true leader faces this in his struggles and must be unmoved by such things. If not he and his men shall fall to the jaws of despair."

"I'm speechless. I know that you're right, Sir. Logan. Thank you so much for your words. I only want to help others, I really do, and I hate how powerless I am. I hate the fact that I could not protect my mother, my father, my friends, and now Aleya, the person I care for most might be a slave, while I'm here training and living freely." As I spoke tears began to flow from my eyes. Despite me trying to hold them back, all my emotions surfaced.

"Orion, no man is truly free. We are all slaves of something. I to the endless search for knowledge and you to this dream you hold on to. We believe we bear no chains, that we are free in this life, yet we all bear the same shackles, made of flesh and bone, never able to grasp the beyond," said Logan as he held me.

"I'm sorry, I'm so sorry. You must think I'm a coward for crying like this. I always say I'll be a knight or a leader and yet here I am crying like a child."

"It's fine. I've seen the strongest and bravest men cry. I've seen the wisest men fail and the most powerful powerless. I see within you a truth that's rare. I've only seen those eyes once in my life, Orion. I once knew a man who sacrificed everything for those he loved, a man who fought against all the odds despite having nothing. This man also desired to help others, and the more he struggled the more pain came to him, as if a test from the creator itself. However, he was consumed by life, and all of its trials. Sometimes life pushes you to the point of no return, and I watched this man fall into the abyss. You see, the world took everything from him, leaving behind a mere husk of who he once was. It saddens me to see such good men feel such pain. It seems life favors chaos for some reason, and so I, too, have vowed to make a change. So believe in me, you're not alone. We have all lost and we have all dreamed of a better tomorrow. Just keep your dreams alive, no matter what happens."

Cleaning my face I stood back, "Sir. Logan, thank you so much, I'd never stopped to think about others. I know everyone has their own past and it's strange but it helps me feel understood. Thank you."

"Life has a funny way of taking what we see precious from us, in order to set us on a path. Some would say this is divine intervention, but I'd say it's a mockery of our existence."

"What do you mean, Sir. Logan? A mockery of our existence? Do you mean to question the Creator's plan for us all?"

"Orion, are you familiar with the religions of the lands?"

"Honestly no. I've heard father read text from the Holy Book but never had the privilege to read it myself or attend the ceremonies of a cathedral."

Logan smiled. "I see, the youth always keeps such ideals hopeful, especially when they haven't seen what it does to man. I'm not against the holy scriptures per say but more so the men who use it to control and deceive people. The scriptures speak of a Creator of all existence. This creator has a plan for each one of us, and so I sit and ponder at times what kind of plan involves the death of millions, the torture of countless, and the rise of great evils through history. It baffles me, but that's why I turn to alchemy. You see, we alchemists do not leave it to faith but rather proof. If there's such a creator watching countless suffer as such, then I shall make it my mission to change such a cause with my own two hands."

His words were truly powerful. "Sir. Logan, I'm sure that if anyone would hear you speak like this they would see it as blasphemy. I'm not an expert but it sounds like you wish to challenge the Creator?"

"I'm sorry, Orion. I didn't mean to sound as such. If anything I got carried away. However there's a story I'd like to share with you if you have time. It's an old story I once heard."

"I have time, Sir. Logan."

"Tell me, have you ever heard of the Ashen war?"

"Once father told me that long ago there was a great war between Bartholomaios in the north and the other kingdoms. He said that the north was full of greed, and that there was a man with the lust for power who waged war to try and take all kingdoms. Nigh also mentioned some details of history, but it all seems confusing. I'm not sure what to believe about those stories."

"Well, every story has different sides. History is never such a clear thing. I'll share with you some of what I heard through my days as an Alchemist. Before we begin, tell me Orion, are you familiar with the lands and its kingdoms?"

"Well, kind of. I didn't spend too much time learning of the lands when I was young."

"Well, to make sure that you grasp the picture of what I'll tell you, I'll help you better understand our lands. Here in the south we stand within Stein also known as Stein's Fortress, for its thick walls that were built in the times of war. To the east is the golden kingdom of Alluvium, the center of power and politics. To the west is Minaria, which I am sure you're familiar with seeing as the south and west trade often. To the north is Bartholomaios, the ashen kingdom."

"Yes, I was aware of the kingdoms. Sorry I should have just said it."

"Well, seeing as the stories of the past can go between one thing and another I wanted to refresh your thoughts."

"It does help, thank you Sir. Logan."

"So now that we're acquainted with the lands, let me tell you of the past. It all began over a hundred years ago before the Ashen war when there lived a man in the north by the name of Samael. Many said he spent his days seeking the meaning of life. However, the more he understood the more questions came to mind, and over time he had reached the point where he could prolong death for those who wished a longer life. In those days the north was known to have grown tremendously, as it quickly became the wealthiest of all kingdoms. Minaria and Alluvium paled in comparison to the north. Stein merely stood as farm lands, never with a desire to grow beyond its commodity.

The north, on the other hand, built machines that would help them with day to day activities allowing the people to complete tasks much quicker. Some say that they even used alchemy to turn lead into gold, or other metals into the majesty metals known as silver and gold. All these advancements came because of Samael's thirst for knowledge, a man who had given himself entirely to the search for knowledge. Soon enough people began to say that the north used dark arts that mimicked the Creator's power. The word spread through the land and with it came judgment, as the kingdoms questioned the north and their ways. A summit was called forth and the ultimate decision was to strip the north from these machines, and all known to aid them in such ways that helped them with their daily tasks. War was looming over the land because of this strife. It was the beginning of the land's darkest days."

"But everyone has always said that the north were just heretics, who worshipped false gods and brought about a plague."

"Like I said, there are many stories, but actually the north desired peace above all things and so they complied with the demands of the others. However, after doing so they cut their ties with all the kingdoms, and in their pride they cultivated their own monarchy that stood apart from all the kingdoms. Years passed and Samael, the man who sought knowledge, had been stripped from his alchemy by the people as a safety procedure, despite him devoting his life to the north's wellbeing. Soon after he came to a harsh realization as he saw those he loved turn on him. After years and years of aiding many who were sick, he found himself powerless, at the hands of an illness that had no cure. The illness did not threaten his life but rather his heart, for his wife had fallen victim to a rare disease. The disease would slowly turn the skin a pale color soon resembling a silver-like glow. The eyes would turn a pitch black color, and the hair would grow as white as snow. The man struggled for a cure, but to no avail, and he had to watch his wife suffer each day as the disease slowly ate away at her skin. As she slowly lost her eyesight and ability to speak with clarity, she found herself unable to even reach out to Samael. Each day she screamed in agony, each day she scratched her skin until blood dripped from it as she begged for death. But the man could not come to it, as he loved her more than life itself. Vowing to save her he formulated a medicine that could numb her pain for a prolonged time, allowing him to have peace of mind. Knowing that she no longer suffered he soon set out to the west, as he'd heard of a man who was called the Father of Alchemy, wielder of the philosopher stone, with power that called out to the heavens and challenged the Creator's existence. The man was said to have formulated this stone or elixir for eternal life. Samael knew that this was possible for he, too, had been searching for the answer, but he had never been able to crack the code. Seeking the Father of Alchemy, Samael soon came across what is said to be the result of endless experimentation. Samael described the Father of Alchemy like a monstrosity. He said the man had no skin, with the legs of an animal and the wings of a giant bat. However the Father of Alchemy proposed saving the one he loved if only Samael would promise to take his place as the Father of Alchemy, for only Samael possessed the knowledge to continue the research. Following this, the Father of Alchemy vanished leaving Samael with his secret laboratory, and two vials of blood. One contained his blood and the other seemed empty, but was said to hold the elixir of eternal life within it. Before leaving, the Father of Alchemy instructed Samael to finish creating what he called the Codex. He explained that the elixir was indeed just a drop of what the philosopher stone was capable of, and that only with the Codex could it be obtained. He explained to Samael that there was an existing stone, but that it could never be obtained again, as within that stone was terrible power. The father said that the philosopher stone would contain all the secrets of life within it, and so it would be humanity's salvation, or utter end. He said he had foreseen a future of tremendous destruction and despair. Maybe it was because man would try to reach the heavens or maybe because we were too destructive that we would just seek our own end. Before leaving, the Father of Alchemy warned Samael of the original stone, for it was to one day awaken in this terrible world. Being left with all this knowledge and thoughts Samael quickly rushed to the north to save his wife, as the Father of Alchemy said that his wife would only be saved with the elixir of life. But that it was one of its kind, never to be duplicated again. Since the philosopher stone could only conjure one of these then it would deny its creation again. The stone contained within it omnipotent power yet it was governed by many rules, and its creation was beyond any man's comprehension. The Father of Alchemy then said that it would take an eternity to reach the truth of the world in order to create the philosopher stone and save the world from the destruction the first stone might bring, and only the elixir would give him that time. So Samael was faced with either saving the one he loved or saving the world from an empty end. The second vile was said to slow aging greatly prolonging life, but at a price, for it was the imperfect elixir. With it a great curse would come to the one who consumed it, and in return they would gain a power beyond man. As he traveled to the north Samael crossed many towns and saw many people as they lived their lives in peace. Seeing all the life that surrounded him he was challenged with the thought of what to do. Once arriving at his home, he could see people looking at him with strange eyes. Making his way to his house he saw his home had been recently burned to the ground. Rushing to the rubble he scrambled through the ashes only to find what looked to be his wife. He had been gone for months and without knowing it she had bared a child to the world. As he looked at his wife lying there holding a baby he watched as the wind took their ashes away. Taking the elixir of life in his hand he quickly opened the bottle, knowing that he just wanted her to live once again. Samael poured it on her lips, but nothing came out. In tears he looked to the sky, as he cried out in agony. Samael looked at the other bottle with the black blood. Grasping it tightly with his hand, he took a deep breath as he felt those he loved drift away with the wind. Looking around he saw all the people staring at him, and with hate in his eyes he opened the bottle, pouring out the blood to his lips, cursing them all to death. 'After all I've done for you, after everything I've endured, this is how you repay me, with death? Then let death be our escape from insanity!' As the last of the blood poured out to his lips a black pool of liquid built beneath Samael's wife, and from there what looked like hands began to grow as they began to grab everyone, also pulling her. Scrambling towards his wife Samael tried to get her away as they pulled her beneath but the more he tried to pull her the more hands grew from beneath the ground pulling her in. Samael's arm was torn apart by one of the hands, as it quickly regenerated. Shocked, Samael grabbed his arm, realizing that he was the one who had consumed the elixir of life. The Father of Alchemy had lied to him and led him to believe one vile was the other. Looking upon his wife's eyes as she opened them with fear, she begged Samael to save her. But without a moment's passing the hands completely covered her and the liquid spread all through the land of the north, and with it all those who lived had been taken under. Left in a pool of blackness Samael watched as everything he knew vanished. Looking at his hands he could see nothingness."

Sir Logan stood with great inspiration in his eyes, as he had told me a story I had never heard of before. I stood in silence. The story made me feel somewhat uneasy, yet it all felt familiar.

Turning away, Sir. Logan said, "In the end whether stories such as the one I told you just now are true or not, the lesson to be learned is that we should all seek a greater truth, for we never know what hides behind what we seek. As you can see, great pain has come to many and sometimes that pain leads us to a greater truth or a darker path. It all depends. Sometimes the greatest of truths linger in the darkest of places."

"The Father of Alchemy deceived Samael. It's truly sad to hear a story like this, but could it have been real?" I asked.

"The Father of Alchemy may have deceived Samael, or maybe there's more to the story. One never knows the truth, and the reality may not be as such but the man Samael existed. Of that I am sure."

"You know, there was something you said that caught my ears, Sir. Logan. You said that his wife had silver skin, black eyes, and white hair?"

"Yes, this was the trait of the Ashen, that's why it's called the Ashen war. From the north a legion of Ashen marched upon all kingdoms, but that will be a story for another time."

"Yes, but before we go I wanted to say that I've seen someone that looks like that, in a dream that is."

"Hmm, is that so? Do you know who this was?"

"Yes, it was Nigh. He was kneeling down, holding his sword, and I could see him change into an Ashen. I didn't know what it meant in the moment, but now that you mention this, it sounds familiar."

"I see. Well that's rather interesting. I'm sure it means nothing. Maybe you've heard this story before without knowing you have, but try not to speak of this much, as people are rather skeptic of anything beyond the norm. I'm sure while training with Nigh he has told you to keep many things to yourself, and it's wise that you do so. Well, now I must be on my way, and you too should try and get some rest. I'm sure you're excited for your upcoming graduation."

Walking away Sir. Logan waved goodbye.

"Thank you, Sir," I said as I turned back towards my room. It was late and I had to get to bed, for tomorrow I would meet with Nigh for training. Making my way back to my room, I continued to think about the story of Samael, a man who had given everything for the one he loved and still was unable to save her. Sir. Logan seemed very passionate of the story as if he shared the same loss. I too have lost much, and so I understand the sense of loss within Samael.

Finally reaching my room I laid in bed, once again staring at the outside. This time I could see the moon. Without a single cloud in sight I could see the moon clearer on this night than any other night. Taking a deep breath, I thought to myself, *What happened to Samael? Could he have actually existed, and if so then what happened? Did he die? Or is he still alive since he is the one who consumed the true elixer?"* I knew that the north had been a rebellious kingdom that stood against all others and for that they had been completely destroyed by the other kingdoms. Father told me stories that the north had tried to poison the others and then had risen an army so large that all other kingdoms had to stand together against them. But what was the truth? Was it what I had heard as a child or was it what Sir. Logan had spoken of tonight? Tomorrow I'd ask Nigh. Maybe he knew a bit about what happened back then.

Thinking to myself about the story Nigh had told me I could not help but question the story Logan had just shared with me. It seemed that there were ties between both, yet many things did not add up. I wondered if the Father of Alchemy was one of the brothers that Nigh mentioned in his story? And if so why did Logan say that the Father of Alchemy had become a monstrous creature? Could there be some truth to this story if they tied in like this? But what of the other brother? What of the artifacts? And the hero of the Ashen war? All of this history seemed to be a great part of our lives. I wondered, *what is the goal of*

*alchemy? Is it really to reach a power that rivals that which created us? If so, with a power like that, a man could rule all the lands and be king for eternity. That would allow him to bring war to an end and create a new world where man could live in peace. I must learn more of this. I hope Logan will tell me more, or maybe Vivian. I know she, too, is an alchemist. But now I see why it is so frowned upon. Just a few conversations with Nigh and Logan and it has stirred thoughts of eternal rule within me. Maybe we were not meant to wield such power. However, what justice is there in all this senseless death? And if we have the chance to obtain such power why not wield it to create a better world for ourselves? But would someone be able to wield that power and actually control it? Or would it consume them?*
With a restless mind, I quickly grew tired and closed my eyes, while I tried to imagine Aleya, "It would have been nice had I truly been able to see her tonight."

The following day, waking up in a rush I realized that I had overslept, but as I walked in front of the mirror I realized the same shadow in the corner of the room stood as tall as the roof. But when I cleared my eyes to look, it was gone. The figure was the same as I had seen before. Whatever this thing was following me, it was showing itself to me more frequently now for some reason. I did not feel fear from it, rather curiosity as it called out to me. Suddenly I remembered the night that everyone had died in the town I had seen the same figure bow to me. Stunned by what I had just realized I stood still, when I heard a knock. Opening the door, Nigh stood with a face of anger.

"Orion, we're all waiting for you. Why are you so late? Today is the exam to enter the last phase of knighthood and you're already late," said Nigh with an irritated tone.

"Sir. Nigh, I'm sorry. I've been having a strange morning."

"Is that so? Well make your way to the grand hall. We don't have all day."

"Yes, I'm on my way," I said gathering my things quickly.

Making my way downstairs I noticed everyone looking at me with an angry face, as they all stood in formation. Rushing to the back I stood next to one of the trainees. Putting my helmet on I heard everyone gathering their things as they readied themselves.

"What's going on?" I asked.

"Shhhh," everyone shouted.

It seemed as if they were waiting for someone very important, and then suddenly Zangar and Oberon who stood at the front of the formation took out their swords. "All hail, King Alantt."

Following their command everyone shouted, "All hail, King Alantt."

I stood still as I could finally see what the king looked like. He was a busy man and few ever got to see his face. Making his way down I saw an older man with long grey hair, fair white skin, deep blue eyes, wearing silver armor with gold engravings, walking down the grand hall. We all stood in awe as he walked closer. We could see his silver armor shining like no other. Looking towards us he nodded his head as if greeting us.

The king stood before the formation as he said, "Today marks the day when our kingdom is blessed with the hearts of those who pledge their lives to the kingdom. Standing before me I see future heroes. Looking past the armor I see young men who have taken a sacred oath to relinquish all fear from their hearts. Standing as true knights of the south I ask thee, young knights, what do you vow on this day?"

The knights in the front formation turned to us, "What do you vow?"

So we all replied loudly, "We vow steel, blood, to give our lives to the fortress, to the stones, to the battle, to the brothers, to the sword, to the king!"

The knights in the front line again said, "What do you forfeit?"

"We forfeit pleasure and power."

"Now tell me what do you desire?"

"We desire justice."

Once we finished we all stood waiting for the king to speak. I could feel my legs shake as I thought to myself, "Is it supposed to be this quiet?"

The king looked straight at me, "You there, come to the front. I wish to have a word with you."

Quickly making my way to the front, I noticed everyone looking at me as if concerned. Nigh stood by one of the pillars behind the king, with one leg up and his arms crossed, looking at me as if thinking what was about to happen. Making my way to the king, I bowed and stood next to him, "Your majesty."

Zangar screamed, "Fool, don't stand next to the king, you aren't his equal."

Placing his hand on my shoulder the king said, "No need to yell, Zangar. The boy has done nothing wrong, for he is my equal, and all of you are. I once stood as a proud knight before wearing this crown. Know this men, what truly makes you a leader is not a crown, nor a title, but rather your actions. You see, a man who leads from the front lines is a true leader, and he must bear the same mark of a soldier on the battlefield. He must never hide behind others, but rather become the symbol of strength and hope. I want all of you to think of yourselves as a vital piece to a greater cause. There is no man here that is expendable, and so I wish to know all of your stories, for the day you follow me to battle I wish for you to do so with passion and the will of fire. No true king can lead a people with mere commands. It must be a silent command, where we all stand as one, where words need not be spoken for there is no need for a true king to bark orders, as his men will follow him to the grave. Now tell me, Orion, what is your story? What brought you to the brotherhood?"

Looking around I stood in silence as I thought about my past. My heart began to beat faster. Closing my eyes I remembered seeing Aleya leaving the village, then suddenly I saw the bodies of everyone scattered. I saw Leon staring at me with the eyes of the dead. Looking back at the king, I remembered what Logan had told me, and how Nigh always pushed me to be strong.

"My king, my name is Orion. I was born on the outskirts of the kingdom, where I grew up with a loving father and great friends. As a child I stared at the kingdom from the roof of my home, always dreaming of the chance to become a knight so that I could help those in need and make a difference in the world. However, it all changed the night my village was attacked by mercenaries from the Blood Hand. They killed everyone I loved and took everything from me. Somehow I survived and the next day I woke up covered in the ashes of those I loved. At my side stood Nigh, the one who saved me and brought me here. Ever since that day he has guided me to wield the sword not just for those in need but for a greater cause."

"And what cause is that?"

"Peace, unity, and common understanding between people from all lands, all faiths, and all colors."

"I see. Well it sounds like Nigh to seek for such a dream. Orion, I'm surprised, after having lived through everything that you still seek this life? I'm sure you burden much already. But as you speak I see the eyes of a true knight. I'm proud to see that Nigh has chosen you as his pupil. I have a question to ask, though. Tell me Orion, did you join the knighthood for revenge?"

"Yes. When I joined all I could think of was to seek out those who wronged me and take their lives."

When I said this everyone was shocked, for in knighthood revenge was one of the things we tried to avoid, for it clouded judgment. It was not to say that it was never to be wielded by knights, for with war came loss, and so revenge would always have its place in the battlefield. However, being a young knight it was something many saw as a bad omen.

"I know this isn't the answer many would want to hear from a knight who's so young, but I speak the truth. When I first entered I did so for revenge. Even when I was a child, I dreamed of revenge. You see, my mother was taken from me by mercenaries as a child, and that's what led me to seek out the dream of becoming a knight. But after training with Nigh, after these long two years, I've seen that there's much more I seek from knighthood, and that I know I can contribute more to the world by seeking the other truths."

"Well said. I'm quite impressed with your ideals. I can see the fire in your eyes and the truth behind your words. It seems you have a difficult path ahead of you, Orion. You seek much more than most and have been pushed by life's circumstances to that point. Who knows, maybe there's something you can do that will make a change. Maybe you can aid Nigh in unifying people as you say. Every man here has the potential to change the world around them. Some may not desire to do so and some may avoid it all together, but regardless, all of you are meant to impact the world in one way or another. Orion is an example of the effects other's actions have on our lives. You see, those men who took his mother's life, those who raided his village, are the ones who brought him before us and gave him this endless will to strive for a greater cause. Maybe because of those unfortunate events many more shall be saved, and that's how he shall honor their lives by saving many more lives in their name. Thank you for sharing this with us, again. Nigh has chosen wisely. You're a prized knight. As all of you are, but I wish for you to look at this young man before you and see that despite his hardships he hasn't lost his sight in the light."

Turning back to me the king asked, "With that said, tell me Orion, are you ready to take the dreams of others? Can you become as cold as steel, and cut the threads of another's life when the time comes?"

Without hesitation I said, "Yes, I shall be the cold steel."

Everyone behind me followed with, "The blood shall freeze upon our hands."

The king said, "We shall see. You all make me proud, but know this, the road ahead is much more difficult than meets the eye."

Walking away, the king patted Nigh on the back and smiled. Nigh looked at me with a smile and walked over to me. "Orion, that was very impressive. We really only spoke of my dream of unity once many years ago when we first rode inside these walls after I found you. I'm surprised you hold on to it as you do. By the way, I know speaking of your past is not easy, and it's good that you've overcome the past as you have."

Looking at Nigh I said, "Thank you, Master. Last night I met Sir. Logan. He and I spoke for a while, and he made me realize a lot of the things you have also pushed for me to learn."

"You met Logan? Well that's good. He's a man with a profound understanding of many things. He and I both agree that the world is divided, and that we should fight to unite it. I wasn't aware he was back yet, but I'm glad he has made his way back here. We need good men such as him in times like this."

Nigh handed me an amulet with the symbol of the south, which was a flame with two swords crossing one another. "You're now a knight. Welcome to the brotherhood."

Everyone started to cheer. They were all happy that they had graduated. I saw Zangar make his way to the front of everyone. "Ok, listen up. Next week we'll have a banquet for our new knights. It's well deserved. You have all earned a good feast."

Walking away, me and Nigh went outside, "I look forward to working with you now. Who knows, maybe we can find a way how to mend the wounds of this world together. For a long time I've sought for a way to unite the kingdoms, the lands, and all the people but it has never come to be. When I was a boy someone very special to me showed me this path, and it has been a rather difficult path ever since, but for some reason I can see that maybe if I fail in my search for this unity, that you shall be able to unite them all."

"You would trust me with it?"

"Why not? I can see no better choice, but don't pry on that. We'll talk some other time about ideals. I must go and see Logan. I'll see you later."

"Ok, sure." Parting ways I saw everyone look so happy. It was one of the best feelings I had ever had, to find myself living my dream. I thought to myself, *This is for you, Aleya, Leon, father, and more than anything you, mother. I know you all are proud of me.*

Walking away, I felt a sudden shiver. Looking in the distance, at the side of a mountain, I paused as something seemed to call to me.

# CHAPTER 4

## BANQUET OF RED

*The year is 1117*

A few days had passed since the graduation and the time of the banquet neared. I could feel the excitement building in the city. Looking outside from within my room I saw people working quickly to decorate the streets. Flowers, large tables, and chairs were carefully placed near the central area. They grinded wood and then placed it on the ground carefully, using it like a canvas, coloring it in order to recreate the success of the blood war. I could see they had already painted what looked like a knight in the center. He stood wearing black armor, with an enormous sword. Surely it was a depiction of Nigh. Strangely they had colored the hair rather light for it to be Nigh and it seemed as if the figure was rather petite, like a woman. But nevertheless, it was quite exciting to see people put in this much effort for our graduation. I had never seen people grind wood to dust, spreading it evenly across the ground as such. It all seemed like a lot of work. Others not painting would make sure everything was clean and perfect for tonight's event. I could smell the food from within my room. It was rather pleasing to smell such delights, from roasted chicken to meat stew. Everything I could imagine was being cooked.

Making my way downstairs I ran into Nigh. "Sir. Nigh, I saw them painting a portrait of you outside, but it looked a little different. If you'd like I can tell them to correct it?"

"No need, Orion. That's not a picture of me."

"Really? But I thought you were the only one who wore black armor?"

"There was another before me, the one I told you about a while back, who taught me about lies."

"I see, so she wore black armor too?"

"Yes, she was the first, the one who was originally called the Abyssal knight, but now isn't the time to speak much of the past."

"I see, well is it always this grand? I mean, this banquet is a great honor to us."

Nigh smiled. "Orion, the way they see it is that you're willing to sacrifice your life for their wellbeing. In their hearts the least they can do is honor you with a banquet like this. They've been preparing for this banquet since you began your training. It's part of the customs in the kingdom, a tradition to honor the newborn knights. They grow specific livestock just for this event, so every bite you take today is meant for you to enjoy. This is how we all share this bonding experience. You see, in a kingdom every person is vital, like the king said. The only way the kingdom functions is if every person actively works on their part. Without the farmer we would all starve, without the knight we would have no security, without the builders we would have no homes, and the list goes on. Never forget that. Now go and enjoy this day to the fullest, because it is truly a great honor."

I stood in silence for a second. "I'm truly honored by what you say. I'm speechless in all honesty. But what you say is true. We all have a role to play, and I'll make sure to honor them by playing my role with honor."

Nigh placed his hand on my shoulder. "Stop thinking so much for today. I must go now. Go and have some fun. I'll be back for the event."

"Ok, Sir. Nigh."

Walking away Nigh turned around. "Oh and Orion, save me some food. I've seen the way you eat."

Laughing, I nodded my head. "I'll try."

Making my way outside I ran into Straif. "Sorry, Sir Straif."

With an angry look Straif said, "You should watch where you go, Orion. Next time I won't be so nice, even if Nigh is your master."

Looking down, I softly responded, "Sorry." I could feel the anger build inside me, as he had always been a rather rude man.

"Now Straif, I taught you better than that. Orion was merely walking, no need to be rude to the boy," said a familiar voice. Looking up I saw Logan walking close to us.

"Sir. Logan," I said with a smile. Looking at Straif I noticed his expression change to one of worry. Sir. Logan's voice was undeniable. It was calm and powerful. Each word he spoke demanded attention.

"Master, I apologize. I was merely teaching the young knight the courtesy he should have for his elders," said Straif with a timid voice. I could see that he was afraid of what Logan would say. Thinking back I remembered hearing Zangar say that he didn't like Straif's master, which meant he didn't like Logan. But why?

Logan walked close to Straif, "I see, so you wish to teach a person courtesy without having it yourself? Straif, what's one fundamental lesson I taught you about humanity?"

"My master, you've taught me many fundamentals, but of which you speak I do not know."

With an angry tone Logan said, "Yes I've taught you many but which applies to this moment? Best I remind you myself before you sully your name any further with foolishness. Orion, take this to heart as well. A man who is in power should never use this power to prey on those beneath him or he shall walk with only the shadows of those he leads. No man desires to be treated like a dog, and no man shall ever desire to follow a man who belittles him. Straif, Orion may have just become a knight. He may have never experienced the horrors of war, or felt the warmth of another's blood upon his hands. But what do you know of this boy's past, nevertheless his future?"

Looking away Straif said, "Truth my Lord, I know nothing of the sort."

"Exactly the point. You know nothing of the sort, so try and be a bit more humble or one day it may come back to haunt you. Now if you may excuse me and Sir. Orion, I wish to have a word with him."

Opening his eyes in shock Straif looked at me, "Sir. Orion?" Looking back at Logan he said with an angry tone, "Yes my master."

Straif walked away, and Logan walked closer to me. "I apologize for his behavior, Sir. Orion, but he has been a rather narrow minded man from the day I took him under my wing."

"Sir. Logan, you honor me by calling me Sir, but I still haven't earned the right to be called Sir. I've yet to even see battle."

"Nonsense! The last I saw you were knighted, and you were to be in my squad when Nigh takes leave to the east soon. If you feel so strongly about it though, then I insist that you just call me Logan. I've never truly seen myself a knight either way, nor do I indulge in such formalities that merely separate us from one another."

"Are you sure, Sir. Logan?"

"Yes, call me Logan. I much rather take titles and place them aside. Like I said, they merely create a barrier between people, and it seems people nowadays create barriers between each other at any given chance. Take, for example, those who believe in the art of creation versus those who believe in the art of reformation. They separate themselves when in truth each one seeks the same thing; both seek a meaning to life and their existence. It's sad to see humanity always divide itself, always so vigilant when it comes to see the difference and always so oblivious to the immoralities."

"Yes, Sir. Nigh speaks the same of people and how they have separated themselves by whatever means they can find. He says you and he agree on the same issues, and he believes that I can be of assistance to help him build a better world."

"Is that so? I'm glad to hear that Nigh speaks such words. He and I may see the same problem but we've gone about fixing it in rather different ways. While he waits for the opportunity to arise, I take charge and create them. You might say that he's a man who believes a Divine power shall come forth, and I'm a man who wishes to make this change with his own two hands."

"I see, and why don't you two work together? Is that not another form of division? Maybe if you two could learn how to see eye to eye you can find a way for others to do the same."

"Very perceptive. That's why I know you're one to do what both Nigh and I have never been able to do. Maybe you can be the one who finds this median between me and your Master, and that can be the solution we all seek. Create a new path, Orion. We're both stuck in our old ways, tainted by our past, molded by our loss, but you're of a fresh mind, still young and willing to fight for the cause."

"It all sounds a bit much, Logan, but I want to help others and never let what happened to my village happen again."

"I believe it'll take some time, but you'll reach this dream of yours. I'll make sure I aid you in this path, my friend, for I can see the truth in what you seek."

"I don't understand. I'm so young and you've yet to see me in the battlefield. How can you place such hopes within me?"

"Call it a hunch."

"A hunch? So tell me, why did Sir. Straif refer to you as Master, and you never stopped him?"

"He refused to ever change that between us, and that's why we're merely master and apprentice, nothing more, nothing less. But you have something much deeper that you seek. I can see it in your eyes, the eyes of a king."

"What? The eyes of a king?"

"Yes, every man has a predestined future, or so they say in creationism, which is odd for me to say because I'm a man of reformationism. But I do agree that the world has a side that we yet do not know of. You see, there are legends of the old days, before the Ashen war, before the rise of any kingdom. In those days man merely sought to live in the world created for him and with joy man lived, but then came a man who was said to unite man beneath one sky. The first king, the one who created the road to kingship. He was the man who created the first kingdom, which now lays in ruin across the blue sea."

"I've heard of this before. Nigh spoke of this."

"The king had many descriptions, Orion. Who knows if he was even mortal, but as legends say the kingdom fell after the king disappeared, and man waged war over his kingdom for ages. Upon waging war, two great leaders rose. They decided to leave the land for it had become a barren wasteland after so many battles. One had two sons and the other had two sons and a daughter. The four men grew to become kings, each with their own passion. The four kings sought out a new land, and came across what we see here today. However, the woman who could not claim kingship stayed in the wasteland, and all of the people left the kingdom of old and came to the new land. Out of the four one of the kings died after falling ill to an unknown disease, and so the other three kings built their kingdoms. The south rose first as the king built the kingdom of wood and stone, then came the west where the king decided to build a larger kingdom with stones and metal. The east rose much later as the king desired to build the most beautiful of all kingdoms, made of pure gold, iron, and stone. Legend says that the east was built by a single man. Because it had taken so long people abandoned him to his dream of this golden kingdom. Now it stands the wealthiest of all kingdoms."

"The story sounds almost the same with what Nigh said, but he says that it was two brothers who waged war using alchemy?"

"I see, well Orion, like I said many stories and many ways to tell them. I can assure you of one thing, there was a king with great power, there was a war of alchemy, and our four kingdoms were built by four men who came from that land. You should seek out the truth within these legends for yourself one day. I believe that you will find something of great worth."

"So what happened to the woman who stayed in the kingdom of Old?"

"That I do not know. There is little to be known about the past, but one never knows what can be found in the darkness of the past. Some legends are true, others are not, and some are made out to be what they are not."

"Yes, I agree, but you still have not told me how this ties into me having the eyes of a king."

"Well, that's where I was leading up to. So there were three kingdoms, and the lands all had a balance, but then one day a man said to bear golden eyes was also said to build a kingdom. Everyone laughed at this and so it is said that the north was built by this man and his brother, but both men disappeared after the great structure was built. Some say that he ventured off to the kingdom of old, others say he died without a single soul ever knowing, but one thing is certain, those who met the man said his eyes pulled you in and made you listen. He was able to lead people with a mere look, and that, Orion is the gift you bear. When I talk to you I feel that there is greatness within you, the greatness of a true king. But with that comes a great deal of burden."

I was shocked to hear everything Logan was saying. "I don't even know what to say. Thank you, Logan. I'm honored to hear you say these words. It seems there is much for me to learn. Nigh is a great master so I truly wish I could train with him still. There's something about his view of things that's truly inspiring. I honestly see knights like you and him and I ask myself, where will I fit in?"

"Orion, don't think much of it. Believe me when I say the time you'll spend with Nigh will be priceless. He's the only man I've ever met who equals my foresight. However, there will be a time when even he, the Abyssal Knight, will need your help. Now I must take my leave. I got carried away with the story and lost track of time. It has been an honor, Orion. May we understand each other's resolve at the end of it all, and may you understand the justice that comes from injustice."

Walking away before I could say a word I stood thinking to myself, *That was rather strange how he said that justice comes from injustice. Well, I should get ready as I'm sure the banquet will begin soon.*

Night came as we all prepared for the banquet. With a clear sky, the evening seemed perfect for the occasion. Knights came to the area and said the king would come soon. With word of the king's arrival we all prepared quickly to make sure that His Majesty would enjoy the evening. It was a beautiful night, with a full moon complimented by the beauty of the stars. Today was a memorable day. Never had I felt such joy in my life. If only those I loved could be here right now.

While looking up at the sky I faintly remembered my father as he always smiled, no matter what the circumstances. Snapping back to reality I made my way to the center where they were setting up the food. The smell was marvelous. I could taste the meat by merely standing close to it. At the far end the others rolled out a purple carpet for the king. The carpet had a golden sword engraved in the center, and it extended all the way to where the food was to be served. The king, a man of wisdom and power, had earned the love and respect of all his people. I could see what an amazing king he was merely by watching how happy all his people were. I barely knew the man but even so, his words were truly inspiring to me.

In the distance I could see Nigh, Oberon, and Zangar walking together towards where we were. Zangar raised his arm high in the air and yelled, "Tonight we feast, we drink, and we sing until all the others hate us for it." Zangar laughed loudly and with a smirk Oberon patted him on the back. Nigh seemed to smile also and everyone screamed, "Yeahhh." It seemed this would be one of those nights I would never forget.

Nigh walked closer to me, "Orion, this is your night. Are you enjoying yourself?"

Looking at him I responded, "Yes, I just have this feeling. I don't know why but my stomach feels tight."

Laughing he said, "Well it's fine as it happens to all men before they take this step fully."

"Thanks, Sir. Nigh. I guess I should just enjoy this night."

"Orion, ready yourself as the king is almost here. The other knights are gathering for formation, so go on and join them."

Quickly making my way to the formation I saw Anibel run close to me, "Nigh, I'm so excited. Tonight we will become knights."

"We're already knights, Anibel. Can you believe it, the king knighted us?"

"Yes, but it only counts after the celebration. Orion, you're always just about business. Try and relax sometime."

"Sure, now let's be quiet, the king is almost here."

Anibel looked forward as everyone fell into formation. Zangar pulled out his blade, "All hail the king."

We all followed with, "All hail the king."

Walking onto the purple carpet the king made his way towards the food. Standing before it he said, "Men, relax. There's no need to be so tense. Tonight is a special night. It's a night for the young that will soon follow us old men down the path of knighthood. Now let's see how good this meat is." Tearing a piece out of the meat, the king bit into it. "Mmm, this is delicious. I have to say this might be why I look forward to these celebrations," he said while he laughed.

We all laughed as well, then the king pulled out a large sword made of pure gold, with a rather jagged edge. "Break formation and enjoy this night, my dear knights," said the king, but as he spoke I noticed a rather strange look in his eyes. Everyone ran towards the food as I stood in place. For some reason I felt uneasy, as if something were wrong. No one else had noticed what I could see but the king had the eyes of a sad man.

Turning around I looked at a man standing beneath a tree. Looking closer I noticed the man was wearing the mask of a jester, as the rest of his outfit was made of black cloth. Walking closer to me the jester smiled, "A night of mad men indeed it is. The beauty, oh the beauty, of it. Well such beauty can be rather barren, if only seen from the distance of the slain."

"What are you saying? Who are you?"

"Names are such a nuisance. All they do is cloud the eyes, branding the flesh, which needs no bounds."

"Your words make no sense."

"I'm the one who makes people laugh, the entertainer. In ways you and I are the same. We show the world something that hides deep within. It's what I do best. A smile is rare these days."

Walking past me, the jester made his way to where the kids sat around and began to juggle fruits. A rather strange man, his words made no sense but it didn't matter. I had to go and enjoy myself. I saw Nigh standing close to where the jester was, so I made my way there, since the jester had peaked my interest with his rather bizarre way of talking.

As soon as I got close to Nigh, he said "Orion, let's go and sit by the king. He's a good man to get to know. Don't think of him as just a king, but also like a father."

"Sure, I mean he looks like a good man, but Sir. Nigh I have a feeling that he's not well."

"Really? What makes you say that?"

"There's something in his eyes that tells me."

"Well, all the more the reason to accompany him."

Making our way to the king's table, we both sat by his chair. I could not help but see the jester still playing with the children, as he would walk and look back, saying "hello" while no one was there. Making his way closer to where we were the jester stood near me and started to make dog noises and pretend to bite his shoulder. "Tell me, what's your name?" I asked the jester as he walked close to me. Without an answer he looked up at the sky, placing his arms to his side as he started to dance. He said, "Just because one can do something does not mean one should."

Nigh looked at the jester and said, "You know, you're rather strange, but I suppose clowns should be as such." Pausing after he was done speaking the jester looked at him and said, "My name is Jester. I'm sure you know this, your entertainer, and you must be Nigh I take it? Well you seem to have great ideas but don't forget that you're a just a knight and ideas are useless."

"Are they now? And why would my ideas be useless?"

"Knights just do things. They don't truly lead. They just follow orders to the end."

"You make no sense, clown. We knights fight for honor, justice, truth, and we have our ideals."

Laughing, the jester said, "You keep assuming. Stop assuming, Master Nigh because you know what they say about assuming. You make an ass out of you and me! Hahahahaha." Despite his irritating demeanor I found his words funny.

"So what am I assuming?" said Nigh with a smirk on his face.

"Well, Master Nigh, you assume you're the representation of good on this earth, that you fight for honor and justice, however have you ever stopped to think of those who you fight against, and how you change their lives?"

Nigh looked at the Jester with a serious look, "Not every life can be saved, but my duty is to my people."

"Is that so? Well then I owe you my life. Now if you don't mind, Master Nigh, I juggle too many thoughts to keep this conversation going. Don't mind me."

Walking away towards the children the jester started to juggle more fruits. For some reason his words kept ringing in my ear. *Who is this jester? And why did he tell me what he did? Why did he approach me and Nigh this way? It doesn't make sense. However what he said makes sense but I know that what I'm doing is for the greater good, or am I just assuming like he told Nigh?* Thoughts continued to pass through my mind as the jester made his way to the knights and set swords on fire while juggling them. The knights stared in awe, but I just wanted to know who he was. Nigh, on the other hand, ignored him all together.

Suddenly knights holding red banners with the same symbol of the south marched in. "Attention everyone, the king's brother has arrived. Salute in honor." Oberon looked at everyone, and standing up we all saluted. Except the jester, as he continued to dance. No one said a word to the clown as he was the entertainer without any discipline. "You may continue to enjoy yourselves," said the king's brother, a rather large man with short red hair and a smile. Walking towards us he sat next to the king.

"Alantt, it has been too long, brother."

"Blake, my brother, what a surprise to see you. It has been some time."

"Well, I sent word before I left from seeing those in the west. Did you not receive the message?"

"No, I hadn't heard."

Slamming his fist on the table Blake shouted, "What? I'll hang the man who failed at this."

"Blake, you'll do no such thing. Such words will not be uttered in my presence."

"Oh, Alantt, I remember now why we've grown so distant."

Looking at his brother the king asked with a stern look, "And why is that?"

Standing from his chair, Blake said, "You've grown soft. A king is a ruler, nothing less nothing more. He must stand above all others. There's no reason for you to lower yourself to the level of these people, as they're here to serve."

Standing from his chair the king said, "Blake, you will watch your tongue."

Walking away Blake said, "Father made a mistake. If only he were here to watch what a king you have become."

The king leaned over to Nigh, "Nigh, it's an honor to see what you all have prepared here tonight." Then looked at everyone who had stood in silence as they had argued. "I'm sorry for the words that have been spoken by my brother. He means no ill feeling to anyone. He's merely unaware of what he says at times."

Everyone smiled and continued to enjoy their time, as the king smiled and sat back down. Placing his hand over his face he sighed. Lifting his hand he looked at me, "You're Nigh's pupil. Am I right?"

"Yes, my king."

"Well, you're a lucky one. Has he told you how we met?"

"No, my king, he hasn't." Nigh looked at the king and turned away.

The king smiled. "Well, I found him outside of the gates of the kingdom as a boy, without clothes, and half dead. All he had was a book. The two men you see over there, Zangar and Oberon, raised him from the moment he arrived here. But the rest are details I'll leave to him. I merely want you to know that you aren't the first or the last who we take in as family from the outside."

The king's words were nice to hear, since I had always felt as if I didn't belong here. Nigh stood up, "If you'll excuse me," he said.

"Before you leave, Nigh, may I ask you to listen to me for a moment?"

"Yes, my king."

Walking closer to the king Nigh leaned over to hear what the king had to say. "Nigh, I've been thinking much these days and something tells me that I must choose my successor soon, and I wish you to be my successor, for my brother Blake is a man of greed, and his ways are far too ruthless. You, however, are a man of peace who desires the wellbeing of others above all things. This kingdom, no the people of this land, need such a figure. You will act as a beacon of light in these dark times."

Nigh looked at the king in shock "My king, your words honor me, but if I may most humbly decline, my king." Bowing down he awaited the king's response.

"Does my decision not please you? I've seen you grow into the man you are today, and if I would have ever been blessed with a son to be the heir to my throne it would have been you. I shall allow you to think of this, so that you may think deep, and so that you may see what I see. Nigh, in you I see a true king. Man needs guidance for man is lost. The times have grown dark, and the old ones no longer answer our prayers. Humanity is in a time of dire need for a good king to guide them. Be that man, Nigh. Be the king I was never able to be. Give hope to this kingdom and share this hope with the world."

I sat in shock as the king told Sir. Nigh to succeed him, yet Nigh did not seem to desire it. I did not understand why a man would not desire the throne. Why was Nigh just standing there in shock? I watched Nigh close his eyes and take a deep breath, as he looked around, and then back at me.

Looking at the king, he said, "My king, I find great honor in your words, I truly do, but I cannot. What I desire, my king, is to unite people, not as a ruler, but as one of them. I wish to bleed beside my men and walk amongst the crowds. I do not wish to be the one that judges them but rather the one that stands by their side while they are judged. The unity I desire does not require a crown but rather the lesson from one man to another. People do need guidance, but they do not need to be ruled by another as is such with our ways. I devote my life to you because you are a true man of honor, but not just because you are king of the south. It is not the crown I kneel to but the man. As for me, my king, I would desire people trust in me as the knight I am not a king I am not."

The king reached over to Nigh. "Nigh, this is why you must be king above any other man. Did you ever hear the entire story of how we met? Tell me, do you remember?"

"Actually, my king, no I do not remember how we met. I don't recall much of my life. In fact, I never think about it. All I know is that I woke up one day here, Oberon helped me walk, and from there I met you, my lord, and you made me a knight with a special exam challenging Zangar. Oberon then became my master and the rest is a dark history for our kingdom."

"Yes, Nigh, the rest is the darkest of histories for our people, for that is when you became the legend you are today. All the men see you as the one who saved the south from the alliance of the Blood Hand factions. You see, not only have you proven to be this kingdom's salvation in the past but you have no desire to rule over people but rather help them. I'll never forget what you said to me so long ago when I asked you if you would choose vengeance or justice and you told me retribution, always following a path beyond us all. But, I suppose some time will be given to you for your decision, and as for how you came to our kingdom that will be for another day. I'll let you enjoy the rest of your night with your pupil."

Bowing once again, Nigh said, "Thank you, my lord. May you too enjoy the remainder of this festival. Orion, let us go and see the others."

But as we walked away I saw a figure standing in the distance near the trees. I could not see who it was because they stood in the shadows. Walking closer I heard everyone say, "The king, what has happened to the king?" Looking back me and Nigh saw as he began to fall, rushing towards him.

Nigh ran with great speed. Catching him before he fell, I saw his eyes roll back as he began to convulse. Looking around for medical aid I saw Oberon rush in with the doctors.

"Nigh, what happened?" asked Oberon as the doctors helped the king.

"I'm not sure. Good thinking rushing for the medics."

"Yes, they always stand near whenever there's a banquet so I rushed for their aid."

Nigh looked at the king in confusion, "What is this? He has never done this. Oberon we must see to it that he makes it to the facility in time. Go and find the crimson knights and tell them to keep him guard. Orion, go ahead and make sure the facility is aware of the situation."

Rushing ahead I saw the dark figure suddenly disappear. It was strange how this dark figure just vanished, but I could not bother with that now as I had to reach the facility. Once I reached the facility I entered, only to find that everyone had been killed, the bodies laid mutilated, torn to pieces, as if crushed by a great force. Blood had been splattered all over the walls. As I walked further in I could feel the blood drip down on my shoulder. As I looked up I could see the ceiling had bodies embedded in its crumbled stone, as if something had pushed the body inside it. Finally reaching the end I felt a sudden surge of cold wind. In this instant I stopped to look around only to find Logan standing in the middle of the room dressed in crimson armor, holding the corpse of a woman as he bit into her neck. Looking up at me with a bloody face, Logan turned his face, his eyes bright red, as veins could be seen from his pale skin. He looked at me as if ashamed.

Slowly walking closer to Logan I looked around in disbelief, "Logan did you do this?" I saw him take a deep breath in, and as he released the air I noticed a faint red mist leave his lips.

"Orion, what you see here may seem like I've committed a heinous crime, but my dear friend, it isn't what it seems."

His words puzzled me. For some reason I believed him, but the more I looked around the more terror I saw in the eyes of all those he had killed. Looking back at Logan, I noticed as he slowly placed the body on the ground that his hands were a darker silver color. As they slowly turned back to their pale color, he walked closer to me.

"You look afraid, Orion. I've little time to explain what you see. I'm sorry, but soon the others will come. I must leave this place."

Thinking back to when Logan and I first met, I saw that there was something he had always kept from others, but never had I imagined that he would bring such death, capable of murdering his own people.

Unsheathing my sword I took a deep breath. I felt my hands tremble in fear.

"Sir Logan, I cannot let you leave this place. You've taken the lives of so many. I can't just let you walk away. I was afraid you'd choose this path, but in truth I cannot blame you, for you know not who you serve."

"Orion, if it means anything, I truly believe in the world you seek, all that you desire, and all that you shall obtain. Death must not come for you today, so draw your sword against me, as I shall not draw mine against you."

With trembling hands I felt the urge to run away. I knew Logan was a man of great power and that I stood no chance against him, but if I ran, what kind of a knight would I be? What kind of king would I become? Biting my lip I screamed with anger and rushed at him with all my might. Instantly I felt my sword pierce his chest. Looking up at his face I noticed his eyes look down at me with sadness.

"A good strike, my friend, the heart is what keeps us alive. It's a symbol of life, and love for those who believe in such things. But I lost both a long time ago, and many years have passed since I last heard the beat of my own heart or the warm feeling that comes with that which you know as love."

Stepping back the blade slowly revealed itself, as it appeared to have melted slightly. Turning away, I looked at my sword in disbelief. As he began to walk I stood paralyzed as he had just been pierced through the heart and without flinching walked away. "Logan, why, why did you do this? Whyyyyy?" Dropping to my knees, I failed to understand why he would kill his own people and not even care for their deaths.

"Because this is their destiny, their greed knows no bounds, their lust for power has corrupted their hearts, and so I must be the one to guide them. Maybe I can guide them to that dream of yours, that kingdom you seek."

"Kingdom? What do you mean?"

"I've told you that your eyes are the eyes of the one who seeks kingship."

After Logan finished speaking I saw an arrow pierce his neck, following by five more that pierced his body. Logan stood in silence, as I heard him chuckle. "I see you all have come before I can leave, however none of you are destined to take the throne, so you all shall perish for these wounds."

Lifting his hand I watched the six knights that stood behind me lift in the air as Logan said, "Be gone." Their bodies were crushed by some sort of force. I heard the sound of their bones and screams echo in the room. Sitting still I looked at Logan as he walked towards the window. Looking back at me I saw his eyes turn a darker red. "Until we meet again, seek the truth that lies deep within this kingdom. When you do I shall come and find you."

Logan jumped down from the window. I did not even stand up to try and catch him. Instead I looked around, thinking about the day all those from my village had died. "Why must death be the only answer?"

"Orion, hey what happened?" said Nigh, his voice coming from outside. I sat there in silence, without the words to tell him what I'd just seen. Moments after, Nigh rushed in with Oberon. "What in creation's name happened here? Orion, who did this?"

Oberon walked closer to the bodies and kneeled to inspect closer, "You mean, *what* did this? These bodies have been torn to pieces and not by any weapon. They were crushed by some sort of force. A few years ago, my men found bodies like this near the mountains, but by the time they came to me and we went to inspect them, the bodies were gone."

Standing up, I walked closer to Nigh. "It was Logan, he killed them all."

Nigh opened his eyes, in shock. "What do you mean? Logan? Orion, what the hell are you talking about? He's one of the top ranked knights, and a man of great honor. How dare you accuse him of such a crime! I should punish you for even saying such a thing."

I knew Nigh was highly upset. He had served with Logan in many battles and admired him a great deal. "I'm sorry, Master, but I swear it's the truth."

Oberon walked towards us and grabbed me, "Boy look at me, and tell me it's true."

Looking at Oberon's eyes I saw sadness come over him. He was also hurt by what he had just heard. In a sense Logan was like a brother to them all. But I had to say the truth. "Logan killed them."

Oberon looked away. "Nigh, the boy does not lie. I can see it in his eyes."

Nigh looked at me with anger and then turned to Oberon, "You believe him? So one of the brothers has turned his back on us all? How can you believe this?" With anger Nigh stormed off.

Oberon looked at me, "You've done well, boy. Don't mind your master. Nigh holds this kingdom and all within it close to his heart. He's just hurt to hear such a thing. Logan was an extraordinary knight, but I can't even imagine how he could have done this. For now let's not get into details as the king finally awoke and is well, but this will surely rattle the kingdom for some time. Come now, we must go and see the king, and all the others. I'll have my men clean up this mess, and Orion, you're lucky to be alive. I'm glad that you're unharmed."

"Thank you, Sir Oberon. I truly feel lucky, and I'm sorry, as I hate having to be the one to say this to you all."

"No worries, boy. Let's go."

Walking downstairs I saw everyone looking at me with a shocked face. The king stepped forth from within the crowd, and walked close to me. "Orion, come with me, we must speak in my chambers. Nigh you come as well, and Oberon, make sure you meet us there soon as well. We must speak of this."

Making our way to the king's chamber I felt afraid of what was about to happen. I kept thinking about what Logan had done and how those men were killed. But how could anyone believe me? It was impossible for anyone to do something like that.

Finally reaching the king's chambers, the king invited us to sit at his table, "Sit, we must take a moment to relax before we talk about tonight, for it has been a night that will surely bring our kingdom under dark times unless we get to the bottom of this."

We sat in silence as everyone caught their breath and looked at each other. The king stood and walked to a cabinet. Opening the cabinet he brought out four glasses and some wine. "I shall serve us some drinks. I'm sure all our minds are riddled with questions, so let's relax our thoughts. Wine always helps me relax, and I hope it does the same for you."

The king served us wine and sat back. Nigh leaned forward and asked me, "Ok Orion, let's start with what you have to say."

"Yes, Master. Well I walked in and saw Logan standing in the back of the room as he held one of the bodies in his hands. It seemed as if he had bitten the person, but I couldn't really tell. He then dropped the body and told me that he wouldn't hurt me, but after he said that six men came in and as they'd seen what he'd done they shot arrows at him without warning. He then lifted his hand and when he did their bodies were crushed instantly. He then jumped down from the window and I just sat there."

Nigh took a gulp of the wine. "Are you sure that is all? Is there anything else that happened? Did you try and strike him or confront him in any way? Or did you just quiver in fear?"

Oberon looked at Nigh. "You shouldn't be so harsh on him, Nigh. He's just a boy."

"Oberon, the boy needs to grow up one day, and he must see that a knight can't just stand around while those he has sworn to protect are being slaughtered."

I took a deep breath and told Nigh, "Master, I'm sorry. I can't recall but yes I did try to stab Logan. But when I did he just stood in place, and he didn't avoid the stab."

Oberon turned towards me. "Where did you stab him?"

"The heart, but he just stood there."

They all looked at me and then at each other. Nigh said, "Orion, it's hard to believe this story. No man could survive being pierced through the heart, and in all my years of war never have I seen a man crush the body of six men as you say. It's absurd."

The king stood up, "Nigh, take a moment and try to listen to the boy. I know you must be hurt but don't allow your emotions to cloud your mind. I believe Orion. What he says may sound untrue to the ears of many but I've seen such things in my life, and so I know this to be true. This discussion will not leave this room. I must look into the matter, and Orion, please do keep this to yourself. None must ever hear of this, and I mean ever. If word got out that one of our knights had done such a thing, it would destroy our kingdom, and all the other kingdoms would look down upon us for having one of our own commit such a crime."

Nigh stood up, "My king, if I may, I've never heard of this and I'd like some answers. I know of relics that give men powers such as control over fire and such but none that make a man immortal. Such things should not exist, and Logan possessed no such artifacts, if not my blade would have sensed it."

The king placed his hand on Nigh's shoulder, "Nigh, there's much that this world hides from our very eyes, and just how you can summon fire with your blade. There is one such thing I have heard of that can give man such powers, to grant man immortality."

"Do you speak of the philosopher stone?"

"Yes."

"But that's just a legend."

"I thought so too, but I've heard that long ago in the alchemic war, when our kingdoms were built, a man known as the Father of Alchemy was said to have created the stone. It ties in with the stories of the two brothers who waged war with one another and the story of the four kings, but I'd never believed such tales until now that we see this. I believe the stone requires life to exist, or so it seems from what Orion is saying. If Logan doesn't possess the stone then I don't know what power he wields."

"I've heard of these stories as well, but one thing is reading a story, and another is seeing it unfold."

"Yes, I know it must be a lot, but now I must speak with Oberon in private. If you and Orion may step outside please."

Nigh bowed. "As you wish, my lord."

We both walked out. Nigh stopped me and said, "Orion, look, I'm sorry. I might have been a bit harsh with you. It wasn't my intention, but I fight for my brothers, and if it would have been you in his place I'd defend you all the same."

I looked away and said, "Master, I thought you kept your sword a secret? Even from the king."

With a smile Nigh said, "Well yes, he doesn't know the full extent of its power. I've shown just the flame that's common, but never the one I showed you."

"Well then why is it so hard to believe what I was saying?"

"Honestly it's not hard, I guess. I just wish it wasn't real, but Orion I must go. I need some time to think. You should go and rest and tomorrow we'll talk."

Making my way to my room, I rushed into bed. Taking a deep breath I closed my eyes and saw Logan's eyes piercing through me. "Why Logan? Why did you do it? And what does he want me to look for in this kingdom? What does this all mean?" Closing my eyes I felt my tired body drift into sleep.

# CHAPTER 5

## BENEATH THE SKIN

*The year is 1118*

*It has been a year since the banquet, since Logan was branded a traitor, and since the king no longer looked upon us, the knights, with the same eyes. Nigh has been uneasy for this last year. His eyes are no longer those of a compassionate man but rather that of a vigilant knight. Looking back to this year that passed, I feel as if it were all a blur. The people went about their lives and the knights continued to train but there was something missing after that night. Along with the disappearance of Logan, Sir. Straif could not be found, but that should be no surprise since he was the student of the man who had murdered the crimson knights. In all this time I had never seen the dark figure again. It seemed it would only come forth when there was danger around.*

Opening my eyes, I watched the sunlight stream through the window. Lifting myself up I looked around my room and paused. "Today will be a good day." Stepping out of bed I went to clean myself before the day started. As I made my way to the baths I looked at Anibel, and she smiled at me, walking closer to me.

She whispered to me, "I want you, Orion." Taking her clothes off, I stared at her body. I felt drawn to her, irresistibly wanting to hold her closer to me. Her body was beautiful, her skin smooth, her figure perfect. Leaning closer I began to kiss her. My lips could feel her tender skin. But as soon as my lips touched her lips I woke up startled in my bed.

"What was that?"

I sat in my bed thinking about her, and why I had just had that dream. *Did I not notice and maybe I had grown fond of her? I wonder?* Making my way outside I gathered my clothes and made my way to the baths, where I happened to see Anibel.

"Hey Anibel," I waved.

She looked at me and without even a smile waved and continued to walk. I paused and looked around. What had just happened? She seemed upset about something. I continued to make my way to the baths. Then I stood with my bucket of water and scrubbed my body as I kept thinking of Anibel, and the dream I had.

Once I had finished I made my way back to my room and gathered my armor. Today I would once again patrol the outer city until the sun came down, and then I would be done. I never knew how boring it would be to be a knight. We had spent the last year patrolling up and down the roads. But this year it had been said that some of us will get different assignments, and some will go to the outer areas, where there have been reported sightings of bandits and even Blood Hand members. My goal was to be stationed in one of those posts, so I could act as a knight not a guard dog.

Finally making my way to gather food to eat, I stumbled across Oberon and Nigh as they, too, made their way to get food. Nigh, as always, seemed a bit distracted as Oberon laughed and joked by himself.

Looking at me, Nigh said, "Good morning, Orion. How are you?"

"Good, Master. Just getting some food."

"Ok, after that meet with me we need to talk about your new assignment."

With excitement I agreed. "Yes Master, I'll see you soon after."

I quickly made my way around and gathered meat, eggs, and rice, with fruits, "This is the best part of being a knight, we eat like kings each day." Sitting down I started to eat fast, but then I noticed Visan, Adriel, and Anibel come and sit with me. Visan looked upset as always, and just said hi. Adriel smiled and tossed me a slice of bread, "Here man, take it," he said.

Anibel sat down and tried to fake a smile, but it was obvious she was unhappy with something, so I grabbed her hand, "Hey, what's wrong with you? Why are you so upset?"

Her cheeks turned red as she moved her hand back, "Nothing, I just feel sick."

Visan smiled and said, "She's just upset because her master put her on patrol for another year."

I looked at Anibel, "Is that it? Don't worry, they rotate it every year. We'll all get a chance."

Looking at Visan she said, "I hate you. Why do you have to tell people my business?"

Walking off, she left her food and made her way outside. I got up and quickly caught up with her, "Hey, calm down. He didn't do anything too big for you to hate him."

Looking at me she said with an angry tone, "Shut up," and then she kept walking. I stood still and thought about following her, but instead I watched as she walked away. Looking back at Visan I noticed him smile, with a sly look. *Maybe I shouldn't have agreed with him. He is a bit of a jerk.*

Walking back to the table I gathered my food and walked off. I heard Adriel say, "Nis, where are you going?"

Stopping in my tracks I looked back, "Did you just call me Nis?"

Adriel smiled, "No, I called you by your name. What are you talking about? Who's Nis?"

"Never mind," I said as I walked away. I was sure he had just called me Nis, but it didn't make any sense. Why would he call me that? Finally reaching the courtyard I sat by the old large tree that sat at the center of the area. Here I was able to relax and enjoy some peace and quiet. I watched as everyone went about their business. I wondered, what drives each person to wake up each day to do what they do? Some were carpenters, others blacksmiths. Each person had a different trade, but somehow their eyes were not full of passion for what they did. It seemed that some had simply found the routine in what they do and were pleased with it but not excited. Even the knights did not have that fire in their eyes, but if they did not have the passion then why did they do it?

While looking around one of the blacksmiths noticed me, a rather tall, older man, with dark skin, and ragged clothes. Walking towards me, I saw his tall figure move closer. It seemed after so many years hammering at steel he had built an unusual amount of muscle, which was complimented by his overgrown beard and lack of hair. Finally nearing me he said, "Hey, Sir, tell me, why have you been looking at us all with that funny look? Do we look strange to you?" he said laughing.

"No need to call me Sir. My name is Orion, and no I don't think of you all as strange, but rather interesting. What's your name, if I may know?"

"My name is Brent, but most call me Smith. I crafted the king's armor, so that might make me one of the best smiths you may ever meet," he said once again laughing, as he walked closer.

"That, or a lucky man, but it's an honor to meet the man who crafted my king's armor. So tell me, why do you forge weapons?"

"Well Orion, if I may take a seat here with you, I can tell you whatever you want to hear?"

"Yeah, I'd very much like that."

Sitting down next to me, Brent looked up at the sky, "Well it all started back in the west, in the kingdom of Minaria. My father was a well known blacksmith there, and some say he crafted a blade that could cut through black diamonds, but that's hard to believe, since I have yet to create such a weapon myself."

Looking at him I asked, "What are black diamonds?"

Laughing he said, "Shiny rocks that are too hard to break, but my father managed to make a name for himself and my mother was also a well known writer and teacher. However, one day the king of the west came to our home and requested that my sister be taken to his palace for his pleasures, and father refused. The king was enraged and banished my father, mother, and me from the kingdom. He said if we weren't gone within a day we'd all die. Many say he was merciful, but the bastard took my sister, and we never saw her again. We left the kingdom and while on route, Sir Oberon saw us. He knew my father by reputation and it seemed my father had crafted his sword many years ago, so he helped us make our way to the south. The king of the west ordered we be sent back, I assume to execute us after giving some thought to his backwards mercy. But, under the treaty of the central kingdom we were able to seek asylum here in the south."

I was in shock at his story, "I'm so sorry for your sister. I don't even know what to say. So what's the central kingdom?"

"It seems you've been busy swinging that sword around and haven't read your history, but I'll sum it up for you, young lad. I'm sure you know about the Ashen war, so I'll tell you that after that war, there were only three kingdoms left, the east, west, and south. Each kingdom had suffered great loss but still, a second war broke out. No one speaks of this short war because it was terrible that after such a devastating war men would still wage war for power. But little is known of this war, other than the creation of the central kingdom, which ironically is located in Alluvium. If you ever happen to make your way to the east keep an eye out for two giant towers. The black one is the central kingdom and the golden one is Elysium."

Smith was really interesting. How he knew so much was beyond me, but he sure had my attention. "So what is Elysium? I'm so sorry for asking so many questions I'm just interested in all this."

With a smile he said, "No need to be sorry, so let's see. The central kingdom was built right after the war, as a symbol of equality and peace. Here the leaders of each kingdom would sit and discuss issues in order to prevent a war. Soon after this, there was a small group of rebels that were being led by a skilled man who was never seen. The group eventually caught enough attention that the kingdoms ordered a hunt for them. This is when the east created Elysium, a prison for those who violated the truce of the land. Any group that opposed any of the kingdoms would face the penalty of Elysium. Some say that death is a gift in comparison to what goes on in Elysium. The funny part is that in an old language from across the ocean, this meant heaven."

"Smith, how do you know all this? I've never even heard of other lands, other than in legends."

"Well, let's see. After I came to the south I had a passion for books, and so I read every book possible. Most wouldn't hear this from me, because they merely see the man that beats steel into art, but know this, young lad, each man has a story to tell and one worthy of a poem and a song." Laughing, the smith kept his eyes to the sky.

"Smith, you're right about that. I hope you don't mind me calling you Smith."

"Not at all. If you haven't noticed I'm rather talkative and friendly. People tend to be so reserved and hidden from each other, but that's sad. Not me. I'm not ashamed of my past, nor my passions. I embrace who I am, as I can see you embrace yourself too, yet I feel as if there's much you don't like to talk about."

"You're right, there's much."

"Well, while you think about whether you should talk to me about it or not let me finish my story before I forget. Now where was I? Hmmm, yes, ok, so once in the south father continued his trade. But every night I saw him cry, not of pain but anger. He hated the king of the west, and so one night he ran outside the walls of the kingdom. He told my mother that he'd come back, but he never did. I'm sure he went to save my sister, but some heroes never reach their goal. I'll always think of him as the man who fought for what he believed in no matter what, and I'll tell you he's a true hero who stood for what his truth no matter what the outcome. We always hear stories of the hero who saves them all but never of those who fail, and those who fail usually endure unimaginable hardships, but are forgotten by history. "

"You know Smith, I've always wanted to be that hero; the one who helps everyone. It's funny how you say it because I wonder if I'll succeed, or will I, too, be forgotten in history?"

Laughing, Smith said, "Lad, you have the world in your hands. You're young and strong. Be what you desire, never holding back. Give it all you've got."

"I always do, so tell me more. I have to admit, you're good at telling stories, like most people in this kingdom." His words made me smile with confidence.

"By most, you must mean Nigh. The man is an idealist, but now to continue. Despite my love for books I picked up the hammer. Mother had fallen ill after father's absence for many years. She cried each night and each day. I sat with my hammer and beat steel to the rhythm of her cries as they brought me both anger and pain. My only way to express all those emotions was by beating steel. At times I too desired to go and avenge my family, but I knew I was no hero, just a man with many books to read and many more swords to craft. So, after a few years mother passed and I was left with nothing. In a way I felt more lost than I ever had but at the same time I felt free. I know it sounds sad to say but I felt free from all the pain I felt from her. I wanted her to be at my side, but not like that. Sometimes in death there is peace, and I was happy she'd found such peace."

When Smith said that I thought about my father, as he had died, but for some reason I could not think like Smith because my father had been killed by those men. "Smith, do you ever wish that the king of the west would just die?"

"Yes, every day, but wishes are for fools, lad. One must have the strength to seek for what one desires. I lack the strength and talent that you knights have, so all I can do is craft the instruments for you all to carry out your missions. But know this. After all that tragedy I became well known in the kingdom and was able to craft weapons and armor for all the knights. That's when the king came to me himself and asked me to craft for him the finest armor. After many months of crafting I finished his armor and then all in the kingdom called me Smith. And now here I am, sitting with you, telling you some history and a bit about my story."

"Yes, I see, but looking at you I can honestly say you're not lacking the strength. If anything you should be a knight. I'm sure few could best you."

"Lad, I haven't the heart of a hero as I said, but thanks. Who knows, maybe one day."

"I will say that you've brought a lot of questions to my mind and a lot of answers, as well. One thing I was going to say is that I, too, know someone who lives in the west. She's my childhood friend, and I hope she's well."

"She should be fine. If you ever need it maybe we can see to it that you see her again. Well, it has been nice, but I can see a knight waiting by my shop, so I must go now, but maybe we can continue your history lesson some other time?"

"Please Smith, thank you so much, and hey maybe one day I can do something for you, too?"

"Just use the swords I make with all your might. Take care now, lad."

Smith stood up and walked to his shop, while I sat thinking to myself, *So much to learn about the past, so little time to learn all this. I wonder why the east has the central kingdom by where they are? And this Elysium sounds terrible, yet I'm sure it's a symbol that keeps men from committing crimes. And to know the west is ruled by such a man and that the other kingdoms allow it is truly disgusting. This reminds me of what*

*Logan said when he told me I didn't know who I served. But Smith seems to love the king despite him not saving his sister. I wonder why, but now I know not to look down upon those who go about their day to day activities. Smith might spend his entire day beating steel, but he still finds the time to read and seek out his passion of knowledge. I'd have never imagined his life to be so interesting, but like he said, every person is worth a poem and a song, yet sadly these stories are never told and die with the person. But not me. I will be king, and no king such as that of the west. I will rule for the people. That king should be brought to his knees and whipped to death. He should suffer many more deaths. I wonder what makes a man think he can destroy families just because they wear a crown.* The more I thought about how the king of the west should die, the angrier I became, until I felt a strange sensation around me.

Suddenly I heard a voice whisper to me, "King of kings, take upon thy throne of corpses, and rule for I shall build this in your name."

I sat in silence. I knew it was the shadow that I had seen before. The voice was the same of the past. "Who are you?"

"In time we shall meet, my king. Until that meeting, keep thou eyes upon the throne."

After his last words the feeling had left me. *What is this?* I thought to myself. I could not help but smile. *It seems I find comfort in his words.*

Standing up I walked forward only to see Nigh rush to me, "Orion hurry, go and get ready, we leave tonight."

"What's going on, Master?"

"I have information on Logan. For the past year I've been working hard on this and now it finally has come to light."

A past unforgotten.

*Logan had taken the lives of many. He had betrayed the brotherhood and taken the honor of all those he served with. Oberon, Nigh, and Zangar all had the eyes of men who had not just lost a brother but a part of themselves. Maybe it is because all this time they had failed to see through Logan's deception. Even I felt a sense of loss. He had disappeared and had taken with him what trust I had left. But now was not the time to mourn, nor the time to dwell on his actions, but rather the time to take actions to bring him to justice. So the king set together a team to seek out answers, consisting of Nigh, Adriel, Zangar, and myself. We would be a small team to search for answers that would lead us to the truth of Logan.*

*The heart is our weakness. If we weren't blind by emotion this would never happen,* I told myself as the four of us gathered our equipment to make our way to the outer area of the kingdom. Before we set out the king made his way to us.

"Nigh, may I have a word with you?"

Nigh stepped away and talked to the king away from us all. I could see them stare at me as they spoke. It seemed there was something I would have to hear later. After a few moments of talking Nigh made his way to us. The king waved goodbye and rode back to the kingdom. Adriel walked close to me, and laughed, "Keeping secrets, huh?"

Zangar quickly grabbed him. "Do not speak ill of your king. Whatever business he has with Nigh is none of your concern. You're just here to follow orders."

Adriel looked to the side. "I'm sorry, Sir. Zangar."

Nigh walked close to them, "Enough. Let us be on our way."

So we set out. While riding out of the kingdom I felt a sense of fear come over me, not knowing where this would lead us to. I could not help but feel a need for answers. I knew that I was chosen by the king because I had come into contact with Logan, and Nigh knew him the best. Zangar came instead of Oberon because the king needed him to do something I didn't know about. And Adriel came because Zangar placed great trust in him.

Nigh and Zangar rode ahead. It seemed they, too, had a lot to talk about without me, but while we rode Nigh and Zangar suddenly stopped. Nigh came closer to us and said, "This is far enough, Adriel. Go on ahead with Zangar, and do as he says."

I was confused but Nigh then came closer to me, "We must go our separate ways."

"Yes, Master."

I knew little of what was going on, but it seemed Nigh had changed the plans the king had made. Nigh turned back towards the kingdom. "Orion, you must never speak of this to anyone, not even the king."

I did not know why he had just said that but he was my master and I had to obey what he said, "Yes Master, I won't speak a word of this."

"Good, we'll now ride to meet with someone who'll give me some answers."

While we rode Nigh kept silent, as he looked angry. I could tell he had little trust in many people these days, including the king himself. It was nice to see him place such great trust in me, but what was really happening here? Nigh looked back at me, "Orion, when we get to the area I want you to stay away. I'll speak in private with this person and we'll go from there to where we need to go."

"Master, what's going on? I can't help but ask?"

"I'll explain it all soon. Just do as I say."

"Yes Master, I will."

Within moments I could see someone in the distance, near the side of a mountain where there were few trees, carrying a lantern. Nigh lifted his hand, signaling me to stay. "Orion, stay here."

I stopped and tried to look as closely as possible, but all I could see was a man with what looked like a mask that seemed familiar. As they stood there talking I felt him staring at me, but all I could look at was his mask. When suddenly I remembered, *he was the same man who had spoken to father that night.* When the thought came to me I quickly rode to him. "Master, you'll have to forgive me, but this man needs to give me answers."

Nigh looked back at me, "Orion, stay there. What are you doing?"

"Master, that man is dangerous. Get away."

When I came closer Nigh looked enraged and asked me, "What do you speak of?"

"He was the one who spoke to my dad in the shadows one night and after that my village got burned to the ground and everyone died."

Turning away the man began to slowly ride away, but then a deep voice said, "Nigh, what you seek lies this way."

Nigh looked at me and said, "Keep calm, let's go."

We followed the man, until we reached the side of a mountain, "Beyond here is where the truth of your kingdom lies, and where the truth about the one you call Logan exists."

Turning towards me the man dismounted his horse and walked closer. "What truth you seek lies deep within the shadows of yourself. Seek that truth and you shall find who truly turned your village to ash."

Enraged I pulled out my blade, "It was you." But before I could strike the man Nigh grabbed my hand, "Orion, stop this."

The man walked away and rode off on his horse, as Nigh looked at me, "Let him go. That man has come to help us."

"Master, do you know who he is?"

"It's a long story, Orion, and now isn't the time, but yes we've met before."

"I know that man is the one responsible. You can't just stop me from avenging my people, Master."

"Orion, you can't act just on your hunch. Stop and think. A knight must be sure of his enemy before he strikes."

"I'm sure."

"Enough. We have much to look into. Still your tongue."

With anger I stood quiet. As Nigh took a deep breath he tied his horse to a tree. Following him I did the same. When we stepped forward Nigh pulled out his dagger, "Orion, give me your hand."

"What? Why?"

"It's an order, that's why."

"Ok."

Putting out my hand Nigh pulled out a book and cut my finger. As soon as the blood dropped on the book, a great force emitted from it, knocking down some trees, and causing my breath to shorten as if the air had been pushed away from us, then suddenly the mountain began to shake. I saw some of the rocks break apart as symbols I had never seen began to light up a bright red color.

In confusion I asked, "What just happened?"

Nigh looked at me, "Remember I told you about relics? Well this book is one of those relics. The man you just saw gave me the dagger I needed to draw your blood to open this."

"Why did it have to be my blood?"

"He did not explain, but he said it was only your blood that could open this door."

"I'm confused. Why my blood?"

"He said we'll find some answers in here. Let's go. We don't have time, Orion."

Walking in, I felt a strong presence within the cave. Suddenly the book began to emit a bright light. It seemed to light up the entire cave.

We walked deeper and deeper until we came across what looked like stairs, which we began to make our way down. As we descended the stairs I smelled a foul stench, making my stomach turn.

"Master, what's that smell?"

Nigh continued to move forward as he said, "That's the smell of rotting flesh."

"What? Are you saying there are dead bodies here?"

"It's strange, but as old as this must be, the smell shouldn't be this foul. The man said this dates back to the Ashen war. Here he explained is where Logan gained the knowledge of Stein. Whatever power Logan has now was obtained here, in this tomb. I wonder where exactly this leads to."

While walking down the stairs I felt as if the walls were moving, as if they were breathing. Looking back at Nigh, I tried to understand what he was talking about. "The Ashen war? But that was over one hundred years ago. How did Logan gain access to this? If what you say is right, only my blood could open this?"

"Well, it seems you're not the only one who possesses the blood needed, but we'll see what we find. The man was helping me because Logan is also his enemy. I'm not sure if I could trust him but he has helped me in the past when I was hunting for an assassin many years ago."

"This is all too much, Master. Why were you hunting an assassin?"

"He took from me someone very dear."

When Nigh finished his sentence, we reached the bottom, where to our surprise we saw a hallway that stretched for as long as the eye could see. On each side there were what looked like rusted cells, the ground moist, and the walls made of strange moldy stone. Looking inside the cells, we saw the skeletons of what looked like adults and children. The adult skeletons had been tied and some of the children's skeletons were hanging. It seemed as if the parents were forced to watch their children die before them.

Stopping for a second I noticed one of the skeletons on its knees, holding something as if protecting it. "Master, wait, this one looks different, and it's not chained up like the others."

"Orion, we haven't the time. Let's go."

Nigh ignored my request and continued to walk, but without being able to resist I walked closer to the cell, only to watch it open slowly. Walking in I saw that the skeleton had been protecting its child. It may have been the mother. Leaning in closer I noticed a letter. The paper was held under their remains, so I carefully picked it up. Looking closer It had been written in a language I could not understand, but it had symbols, similar to those that the man with the mask had. "This must mean something. I must find out what those symbols are."

Walking outside the cage, Nigh stood a bit further down, looking inside another cell, "Orion, let's go. This place is beginning to weigh on me. Never have I seen so many children tortured and killed in such a way."

"Yes Master, sorry. I just got distracted. It's sad to see this, so close to the south. It's strange."

"Yes, it is."

The further we walked the more we could smell the foul smell.

It was so strong I could not bear it, even while covering my nose with my hands. "Master I can't take this. I can't breathe in here."

"Orion, there are worse things than this smell. Now silence and let's move forward."

As we continued to walk we heard the serene voice of a woman, "My, what do we have here? It has been ages since I last saw man."

Shocked, we both stopped. Nigh walked slightly forward. "Who's there?"

"Names are such trivial things. There's no need for further introduction, Nigh. And I see you brought Orion with you. My, my what interesting thoughts linger within you both. One seeks to rule and another seeks to, hmm, best I not say. I wouldn't wish to spoil what's to come."

Nigh seemed enraged as he rushed to the cell. Walking quickly behind him I was surprised to see that it was a beautiful woman. She stood naked before us, with long red hair and golden eyes. Her body was thin and she had fine features and pale white skin. Just the sight of her had both Nigh and I in what seemed like a trance. We stood looking at her, without saying a word.

"Orion, tell me, do you desire me? I can feel your body tense as it burns with desire, unlike this knight who can no longer see beyond the death of that little girl."

"Shut your mouth," screamed Nigh.

"You wish for me to shut my mouth, you say?"

"You heard right. You'll not taint our thoughts with your words."

"Oh my, you make me sound so harsh. I'm merely a defenseless woman, locked away in this forsaken tomb."

Nigh drew his sword as he pierced her abdomen. "Better yet I'll shut it for you, fiend."

The woman shouted as if in agony, but then began to laugh. "Oh my, now this is special. Nigh the most righteous of them all, to strike a defenseless woman. Not very honorable, would you not say?"

"It wouldn't be were you truly a woman."

With a smile she said, "Why great knight? Why does this past of yours bring you so much pain? Tell me! Why did you not save her? When you alone stand above them all, not even kings can attain what you have. But sadly you still do not see what you have deep within you. Pity you humans are always looking to the horizon and never deep within yourselves. But I won't keep you waiting, for the audience you seek isn't with me but rather with another further down. He shall explain what I cannot."

Walking closer to the blade she leaned forward and said, "Nigh, she was a mortal. Why would you be moved by such a creature? They merely seek destruction and chaos. We both know this to be true. They shall never change."

"I don't know what you speak of. I'm also human, unlike you, foul creature."

"Foul you say."

Walking through the cell as if made of air, she came towards me, "Orion, you shall be the key to the awakening."

Drawing my sword I stood back. "Don't come any closer to me."

Turning away she looked back at Nigh as she whispered, "Oh Samael, you're truly a man without end, but this may be the most dangerous game you've played thus far. Yes it makes sense, he too has been fooled, deceived by the most noble of men. How entertaining!"

Slowly vanishing in thin air she pointed at the end of the hall.

"Follow the path ahead, all you seek shall soon be clear."

We both looked at each other as I told Nigh, "Master, how did you know she wasn't human?"

"I once dealt with one like her. I'm not sure what they are, but they aren't human, rather they feed and prey on humans."

"I see. I really think we should leave this place. This is beyond us. I'm afraid we should not be here, Master."

Nigh looked forward, "Orion you're welcome to leave. I must go on and see what Logan was doing here."

"Master, I can't just leave without you. I'll join you. I just don't know what I can do to help. I'm sorry."

"Then let's go. Don't worry, I'm more than capable of protecting us."

While he spoke I kept thinking about what she had said, as she had referred to Nigh as having something no other could have. I wondered what that could be. Even being my master I knew so little, like what the book he used earlier is for. And his past seemed strange, as if he is not who he says he is.

Walking down the hall I could see more of the skeletons. Some were tied in chains and others seemed to have been placed in torture devices. Once we reached the end of the hallway we came across the final cell where sat a man upon what looked like a stone throne, tall and thin to the bone. His eyes as red as blood, he sat trapped by hundreds of chains. Standing from his stone crafted throne the chains began to glow a deep red color. Looking to his side he sat back down, as he then extended his hand, pointing at the book Nigh had.

Nigh looked at his book and then back at the creature. "I can't give you this book. It's our only way out of this place."

The man closed his eyes with tears streaming out, and then pointed to the side where we could see what looked like a small passage near the end of the hall.

Making our way to that area we saw what looked like a laboratory. There were dissected human bodies on tables, decomposing. It was evident that they had been experimented on. Around the bodies were symbols that included six point stars within circles, along with other alchemic symbols, similar to those I kept seeing, both in the letter and on the man's mask.

Nigh looked at me, "This must be Logan's laboratory. What in creation's name was he doing here with all these people, their bodies torn to bits?"

Looking closer I could see that the skin on the bodies was still intact. It was a silver color, and the bodies had ashen hair. In shock I stood still, close to Nigh. "Could it be? Could these bodies be of the ashen?"

Nigh looked at me. "It appears so, as these are the physical features of them, but how? They were alive over a hundred years ago."

"It seems like it, Master, but what does this mean? And what about that creature back there? He seems oddly large and he's bound by strange chains? And why so many?"

Nigh looked at me, "I'd rather not know. That thing seems to have an ominous power, and it seems Logan made sure to keep him locked away."

"But Master, that woman said he had the answers to what we seek."

"Orion, I don't trust her. Let's look around and see what we can find here. I really wish to leave this place. I have a bad feeling about this."

While looking around, I heard a voice echo, "Come, let us speak."

Nigh walked closer to me. "I'll go first. Be careful. If anything run to the exit, do not wait for me, and no bravery. Understood?"

"Yeah, I've got it."

Nigh walked out first and then I. When we came to see, the creature was no longer skin and bones but rather a man with long white hair. Standing from the chair he pointed to the book, "You, wielder of the false codex. Why do you come to this place?"

Nigh said, "We came seeking answers. What is this place? Who are you and why was I told that one of my men, Logan, was here?"

"I know little of the man you seek, other than that he has aided me for many years. I'm what your people call an ashen."

Nigh stood back, "What? But how? I thought you were all dead?"

"Dead you say, ironic coming from you. But tell me, knight, shall you slay me for what I am? I can see the hatred in your eyes, hatred beyond words, for a being you know so little of, merely what fleeting words have crossed your ears. But if so, then do so quickly, as I haven't the time to chatter with ignorance."

"Don't worry, I have every intention of not allowing an abomination such as you to remain, but before I do, answer my questions."

"Abomination? How perceptive of you to say to a man who sits chained by a thousand chains, in a dungeon filled with the corpses of his people beneath the heroic kingdom, Stein. Whose people live and breathe the fresh air of the outside, as they step over our graves each and every day."

"A grave earned by the actions of your people. Now answer my questions."

"As you wish. All I know is that Logan came here many years ago. He found me here like this. I'd been imprisoned by the rulers of the south. I watched as my people were tortured. I saw them take the body of my wife for their pleasures. I saw them torture my son and all those I loved. Each cell in this place was once a life taken by the south by your people."

"Needless to say, how do you know they're my people? I could be from anywhere."

"One never forgets southern armor. Even if yours is different, the smell of the south never eludes my senses. They say that one never forgets the smell of things that have a change in your life. For years your kingdom experimented on us, they found methods using alchemy, the very same thing that all said was forbidden to keep us alive, and gave us the ability to decay very slowly. You see, they had acquired a certain medicine that the north's alchemist had once conjured to save the one he loved to dull her senses. And with that they managed to trap us within our very own flesh. Once we reached the point of death the cycle would begin again. It was a truly horrible end, and most of my people took their own lives after dying so many times. I, however, have continued to die and live again waiting for the conclusion to this tale."

"How so? You said that they found a way to keep you alive and that after death you would rise again."

"In truth it was the conscious choice of death that allowed the potion that they had used to wear off. You see, the mind is what governs the body to live or die. What the alchemist of the north had conjured would force the brain to never allow the body to die, and so the cells of the body would cling to whatever it needed in order to survive.

"I see, and yet here you sit. I take it you have yet to make that choice?"

"Yes, the man you look for, Logan, came across this place after the woman you saw earlier gave him her powers. She guided him here from a faraway land, I believe from Minaria. Back then she swore to us she had found the savior of the land when she brought him here. She claimed that he would understand our pain and suffering even though he was not ashen. It seems Logan had lost much as we had, and somehow had been given a very special gift sometime in his youth."

"Savior, she must have been mad. Tell me do you know of this gift?"

"No, she was the only one who knew."

"And what is that he lost, that would allow him to understand you and your people?"

"All that was said is that he lost his family as a child. More importantly, he lost his brother. When he spoke of his brother, I could see the hatred in his eyes; the eyes of a man willing to go to any lengths to exact his revenge."

"Tell me about that woman we met earlier? What is she?"

"What you saw was merely a thought she left behind, a spectral being who is not her true self, for she died a long time ago at his hands. She, too, was one of the Ashen. You see, women over time gained abilities that defied the laws that govern this realm and so they were killed for it, except her. She came back with a power that rivaled that of the old kings."

"If so, why did she not free you? I've heard those from the old times were like gods, able to create and destroy entire kingdoms at will, but only one of the past was truly the wielder of these so called powers of legends."

"Like her, there was a knight of golden armor from the east with great power. He was the one who imprisoned us here. The knight bearing golden armor was the savior of your people and the end to mine; the so-called hero of humanity that slaughtered all my people to gain his title at the expense of our blood. He is the cause of all of this. He used the relic of time to control us with immense power. He brought terror to our lands and burned everything to the ground. The south would be the ones to keep us and torture us. They wanted to wield what power we had, but never could. One amongst them, with golden eyes, I do not recall her name, was the one to watch over us, and the one to force our bodies to regenerate after death. This cave is completely enveloped in a relic she crafted using the alchemic potion of the north. In truth the very walls of this place are alive. It's all spread beneath the south, slowly bringing to life things that never should be, and all to rejuvenate the body after death, to torture us. To many it was a curse to die time and again, and yet be brought back to life. So we were not fed, nor given water, because no matter how many times we died from starvation we would rise again. After so long I could never see myself as one of you humans. You humans are vile creatures, and so I decided to stay alive, so that I could bear witness to your inevitable end, and after a thousand deaths, I gained something."

Nigh looked at me then back at him. "You speak as if humans are all bad. Tell me, what do you mean by inevitable end?"

"Look around you. Death and destruction consumes the land, barriers of faith, and race, dividing people within the same kingdom. It's all a part of the true nature of man, the seekers of power, the blind ones per say, always waging war in the name of self-made righteousness merely to attain simple things like gold and title."

"I can't argue with what you say there, but not all men are the same."

"If you speak of yourself, know this…you are no more human than I."

"I keep hearing these words and I'll say it again. I won't be confused as to who or what I am. Now tell me, why all these chains? And you said you had gained something? What did you gain?"

Laughing the man said, "Denial, such an interesting trait given to all. Well, that which I gained was uncontrollable. Whenever I felt pain people's bodies would be crushed from the inside and they would die instantly. I never learned how to use whatever I had but, since I had not given in to the pain of death and they soon found it too dangerous to try and kill me, they sealed this place and placed all these chains on me. The chains are said to have been made using the same steel from the old lands, and they bound me to this place."

"You sit upon what looks like a throne? Were you royalty of some sort?"

Reaching beneath the throne chair the man grabbed what looked like a crown. "You might say a man who wears this and sits upon this chair to be king, a royal ruler of me of some sort. I say I am merely an Ashen."

"Merely an Ashen you say. Well I won't pry on your titles, as it matters little now. It seems that if in fact you were once a king, maybe even the king of the north, you no longer have a kingdom to rule."

Looking at Nigh I thought to myself, *How cruel. Why would he say such cruel words to this man? The Ashen may have been the reason for many battles and many deaths, but they are still people and this man has suffered so much.* Walking closer to the cell I said, "Sir, I'm not sure who you are but I'm sorry for all your loss, and if in fact you were king of the north, know this, your people were brave."

Nigh grabbed me with anger. "Orion, step back."

The man took a breath, "Knight, don't grow angry with the boy. His words are refreshing to hear. It has been an eternity since I last heard hopeful words from another, who is not of Ashen blood. Here boy, have this."

The man tossed the crown towards me, but Nigh quickly caught it. "What is this? You think I'll allow you to give him this."

"Why not? All kings should wear a crown. Is that not the customs of man?"

"Not a crown forged in the north."

"Knight, let the boy have his crown. Don't taint others with your hatred. Don't you see it's those young hopeful souls who may yet be of hope in these dark times."

Tossing the crown to the side Nigh looked at me. "Keep your mouth shut. He's an Ashen, understand? They murdered our people in the past. Don't think of him as a friend."

Looking at the crown, I could see the hopes and dreams of the north etched in its broken black steel crown.

"Now with no more interruptions tell me, how did Logan find you?" asked Nigh.

"As you wish. I don't recall much. One day, on the brink of life and death, I was reflecting back on my life before the Ash, before all the despair, when I could taste the soft lips of the one I loved, the one taken from me, and in the midst of it all, I felt a pain unlike any I had ever felt, and so one of the seals placed on me crumbled. It was that day Logan set foot in this place. Through the consumption of our blood he had gained the ability to see what we had endured. After seeing all of our lives unfold before his eyes, after feeling all of our pain, Logan touched my hand and asked me to release myself, to let my pain go. He said he would take all of my pain and power and endure all our pain and suffering as a tool to create an ideal world. He possessed the eyes of a mad man, but maybe that is what this life needs, a man willing to go as far as he needs to serve justice in this cruel world."

Nigh bit his lip. "You speak as if you're so innocent, as if your people weren't the cause of all of this. If it weren't for your people spreading the Ashen plague, if it weren't for the forbidden alchemy your people practiced, we wouldn't stand here. It was your people that waged war against all other kingdoms, when we wanted peace."

Laughing, the man suddenly screamed with anger, "You seem to have lost your memory. I'm sure the history books claim that my people were evil and the seekers of death. But history is never such a simple thing. The twists and lies hidden deep within history are what we should seek. You believe this kingdom to be true, you believe yourself to one of them. You live a lie, knight. The one at your side shall guide you back to your true self, but all in good time."

Nigh pulled out his sword. "Before I set you free of your misery tell me, why was he so obsessed with this place?"

"My misery you say? That misery shall one day be the only hope for this world."

"Misery can never be hope. A world created from such dark ideals shall never flourish."

"Our entire history is written in blood and war, waged through faiths and ideals. Darkness is where we thrive."

"Tell me, why did Logan come here?"

"Because he felt the death and despair hidden within the south. He saw with his eyes what we had endured. You would not understand the feeling of watching hundreds of your people be burned alive, tortured, and treated lesser than human. However, the past has faded and kingdoms have crafted a fable in which the Ashen were demons. Logan saw through the deception and so decided to be the one to change what wrongs were set in motion. I see death in your eyes, knight. You may set me free. I know that you still deceive yourself of your origins, but worry not, the time will come when you shall kneel in the ashes of what you have done and scream out in agony to the endlessness of time."

Nigh put his sword in front of the cell, "In that moment I shall remember this moment." Lifting his sword I saw flames emit from the blade, as his entire body was consumed by the flames. "Orion, leave."

"But Master."

"Leave now!" he screamed.

Running out I felt the heat make the entire place burst into flames. The flames made their way all through the cave, and before I left I heard the Ashen say, "Now we are free." And with these words a tremendous explosion tore the place apart. Finally reaching outside I noticed Nigh standing still engulfed in flames.

"Let's go, Orion," he said, his eyes full of anger. I was shocked at how he had managed to move so fast, and how had he been able to make it out before me.

"Yes Master," I said as we mounted our horses.

Looking at me Nigh said, "This stays between us." Then he pulled out the book and stones and began to once again cover the entrance of the cave.

"Yes Master. I have nothing to say."

As we rode away, I felt something staring at me. Looking back I could see the woman step into the mountain.

"Master!"

"I know Orion. Nothing can be done, let's go."

Finally arriving at the kingdom, guards ran to us. "Sir. Nigh, the king is gone!"

Nigh looked shocked. "What?"

Making our way to the throne room to our surprise we saw Blake, the king's brother, sitting on the throne. With a smile on his face he said, "Well, I'm sure you heard the news. My brother is missing."

Nigh walked closer to Blake, "Yes, and why do you sit upon his throne?"

Blake stood and pointed at Nigh. "You dare speak to me out of place? I should have you wear your tongue around your neck for such insolence."

"I take orders from my king, not you."

"Guards, seize this man."

Rushing to Nigh the guards surrounded him as they said, "Sir. Nigh, please don't resist."

Nigh looked angry, but nodding his head in agreement he placed his sword on the ground. "Blake, what is the meaning of this?"

Laughing, Blake said, "It is King Blake you ingrate."

Angry, Nigh said, "You are no king. Our king still lives!"

Walking down the stairs closer to Nigh, Blake said, "Where is the proof of this? Well?"

Nigh walked forward with anger, "You bastard! Your brother goes missing and this is what you do?"

Blake turned around. "I'll forgive your insolence, Nigh. My brother isn't here and by law that makes me king. Kingdoms cannot run without a king. If and when he shows up I shall relinquish to him his crown again, well after a trial that is, for he left his kingdom without a word."

Nigh looked at the knights with anger. "You bastards let this man sit upon your king's throne. Move those blades away from me or I'll move them." The guards quickly moved their blades down, but the king said, "You're under arrest, Nigh. You're one of the last men seen with my brother, so until the investigation is over you shall be imprisoned."

Nigh walked away as the guards followed. Passing by me he said, "Leave this place, Orion." But before I could walk away Blake said, "Orion, follow them. I prepared a cell right next to your master for you."

I looked at the king. "My lord, but…"

With anger he said, "You fool, know your place. Nigh is a valued soldier, but you I'd skin alive for pleasure. Be on your way. Another word from you and I'll cut that tongue right off."

Turning around two guards waited for me as they apologized, "Orion, sorry about this."

"It's fine. I'm sure we'll be cleared soon."

Making our way into the cells, I could not help but think of all that was happening. We had seen Ashen beneath our kingdom, and found out dark secrets of the south, only to walk back to find our king missing and his brother the new ruler, who was now imprisoning us, saying we had something to do with the king's disappearance. Why did the king leave? And where could he have gone to?

# CHAPTER 6

## PRISON FOR THE JUST

*The year is 1118*

*Honor, the rarest of human qualities. We are such greedy creatures. We have little that holds us together. There is nothing that binds us to one another anymore. The world is ruled by men who are not worthy of the crown, men like Blake. After the incident in the underground caves Nigh and I came to the kingdom and were framed as having conspired against the crown. Weeks have passed, and we have sat here in the darkness. I can feel the madness come over me. In this place they have us contained like sheep, waiting for their answer.*

The hour was late. I kept track of the time by scratching lines on the wall. Since they come and see us every two hours I have kept my mind busy while waiting. Just a few moments ago, Visan was here. He brought us food and water. I can see in his eyes that he couldn't care less about us being in here, but who knows, maybe people believe that we are truly responsible for this.

While thinking I heard the door slam. As guards walked in with more criminals they said, "Oberon, Zangar, we're sorry this is what the king ordered. It shouldn't be too long before we can give you all a fair trial." It seemed they, too, had been framed, and would now join us in this darkness. Nigh had been rather quiet for a long time. He kept to himself, but as soon as he heard that they were to be held in here also, he moved closer to the cell bars.

Oberon and Zangar were placed in the cells in front of ours. Both looked upset but Zangar laughed while saying, "Well, now look at this. We have bled together in the battlefield, brothers, and now we shall rot together in this hell hole." Oberon walked to the back and sat in his cell as Zangar pulled on the bars of the cell, while screaming, "You can't keep me imprisoned with such little metal." The bars slowly began to bend while he pulled.

But Nigh yelled at him, "Zangar, stop. This is what they want. If we rebel they'll brand us traitors for sure. Right now they have no proof. Keep calm, my friend."

Zangar smiled. "Nigh, always playing by the book. Why in hell's name did you let them take you? You of all men could free yourself from this place, and none would dare stop you."

I couldn't see Nigh's face, but I saw that he walked away from his bars, as he said, "Yes but first we have to see what's going on here. I can't just let this happen. This kingdom is falling apart, and everyone is fine with it."

Oberon, while sitting in the darkness, said, "King Alantt left without a single word, but why? We had spoken that day. He said there was something dark coming. He said he felt something within our walls, but he never said what. All he told me was to keep my honor as a knight. Never did I imagine those would be our last words."

Zangar kept pulling until he finally pulled one of the bars off, "There we go, one down, just a few more. Nigh, tell me, the king was talking to you before we left on our mission. What did he tell you? And not just that, you also changed the plans and went a different route that day. Tell me, Nigh, what were you doing? What's going on? That day you told me to not ask you, to just go to where the king had ordered us, but now look at all of this. Tell me, what did you do?"

Nigh responded "Zangar, my friend, now isn't the time or the place for this. We must keep quiet. I'm sure there are guards outside those doors that can hear everything."

Laughing Zangar said, "Nigh, those guards are my men. They'd die before betraying me. I made sure that the guard duty rotated with my men these past few days. Something told me I'd be joining you in this dump. Now tell me."

"Fine Zangar, but, no more questions."

However, before Nigh had the chance to talk, the door slammed open, as Blake walked in. Just the sight of him infuriated everyone. Oberon looked at him while quietly sitting with eyes of a man who would take pleasure in killing him. I had never seen Oberon with eyes so focused on death. The light emitting from the opened door allowed me to see the side of his face. I could feel his patience drawing its end.

Walking closer to our cells Blake said, "There'll be no need for a trial. I've decided you're all innocent, but for precautions Nigh, Oberon, and Zangar you've been stripped of your ranks, and will now join the junior knights with daily duties. I'll not tolerate knights who speak back to their king. As for you, Orion, you shall be placed in the western area to guard. Consider yourselves lucky. I feel merciful today, but another act of rebellion and I shall have your heads on spikes in the center of town."

We all remained silent, biting our tongues. We knew that it was in our best interest to keep our mouths shut. Standing up Oberon walked closer to the cage, speaking with a calm yet sarcastic tone, "Why thank you, oh merciful king of mine. I am honored by your decision."

"I am glad, then it's settled. On with it, I have things to attend to."

Soon after, a group of knights walked in and asked us to ready ourselves, for we would be taken to gather our belongings and make our way back to our living areas. While we gathered our things Nigh looked distracted, as he told Oberon, "We must be careful. Something isn't right here."

Oberon looked at Nigh, "Yes, there's something odd about all of this. They're letting us go so easily. But I swear on my honor, before all this ends I shall have that man's life for all he has done all these years."

Zangar smiled. "This has the scent of blood, Orion. Be careful in that area to the west. I hear that there are increased enemy movements along those areas."

Nigh walked closer to me, and said, "If the time comes, don't be afraid to do what you must to survive. Before all this ends, you shall have the blood of a thousand on your hands. But never fear the choices you make and be sure to always push forward."

"Yes Master, but you say this as if I won't see you or something strange?"

"No, not at all Orion. I want you to be safe, and I know how hard it can be to be branded a traitor of the crown when you just became a knight, let alone all you have seen."

Nigh leaned in closer and placed his hand on my shoulder, "You're a true leader and I'm honored to say you're my pupil. Please be careful in the western areas."

They all made their way out of the room, as I stood in silence with Nigh. "Nigh, what do you mean? I know the western border is the worst area, but you both sound so sure that there'll be bloodshed."

"We're always cautious is all, and seeing how things are going around here, expect the unexpected." Both Nigh and I walked out. As he walked his way I made my way to my room when I noticed Adriel sitting in my room on a chair, staring at the dark of the night from my window. "Orion, I was told you'd be released tonight, so I decided to come here, and maybe have some time to talk."

It was strange, as Adriel had never taken the time to sit and talk to me in this manner. We usually trained. He seemed different, as if something bothered him. His tone of voice was rather down, and serious, somewhat sad. Responding quickly I said, "Sure, we can talk. I'm a bit exhausted, since we've had little time to rest, but if you give me a second I'll clean myself quickly and then we can talk."

I made my way to clean myself, and as I walked I saw Anibel walking. Her eyes gazed at me with joy, as she ran towards me, "Orion, oh thank creation that you're safe." Throwing herself at me she hugged me. "Eww, you smell," she said as she moved back.

Her reaction made me laugh, "Well I've been in that pit for quite a while."

She smiled, "Well, ok, I'll wait for you in your room. I know Adriel said he was going to talk to you tonight. He told me that he needed your advice, but if you don't mind I'd like to sit and talk to you too."

"Anibel, I'll make sure to see you after. I think he has something he doesn't wish to discuss with others, so maybe it's best if you wait in your room and I'll come and see you after."

With an upset face she turned around, "Fine have your romance talk then."

Anibel was always happy but easily upset. "I'll see you later, An," I said as I made my way inside the shower.

Taking a deep breath while filling the bucket with warm water I closed my eyes, trying to relax my mind. While I stood in peace I heard footsteps walk in. Looking back I saw Anibel standing before me, slowly taking her white dress off. Looking away, I closed my eyes.

"Orion, look at me. Don't be afraid."

Opening my eyes, she stood naked. Shocked, I moved back, "Anibel, what are yo…?"

But before I could finish talking she moved closer to me, "Shh, they'll hear us, Orion."

"But, what are you doing?" Without finishing my words I could not help but stare at the beauty of her body. Her skin was a pearl color. Her body was toned from training, and her breasts of a grown woman. Walking closer to me I could not help but look at her breasts as they moved, her legs as they came closer, and her hands as they reached out to me. I had never seen a woman naked, this close to me. She smelled of flowers, and when her hands touched my face, I felt her tender skin, as it caressed the side of my face.

"Orion, take me, hold me, make me yours," she whispered in my ear.

Still speechless and frozen I looked down and saw her toes. As I stared down I could see her hand reach out to my face. She lifted my face and I felt my heart beating faster, as I could not believe that she was still here, before me. Then she came closer and placed her lips upon mine. I felt the warmth of her body, as it pressed against mine, and her tongue caress mine. As she began to breathe harder and harder, my body grew warmer and warmer. I felt a burning sensation as I grabbed her hips and pulled her in closer to me, kissing her neck, and slowly making my way down to her breasts. Her hands held on to my shoulders as she said, "Love me, Orion. Make love to me."

When she said this, I suddenly saw Aleya in my mind, and it saddened me. I had wanted to see her for so many years, but she had been taken from me. Then when my thought left me, I slowly saw her skin turn a silver color. Looking back up I could see it was the same woman I had seen in the cave. She smiled and grabbed my neck, slamming me into the wall.

"Orion, oh the pleasure of your lips upon my breast. I could feel you were ready to explode with all that fire."

I felt her hands tighten as they crushed my throat. "Ugh, what do you want?"

She smiled, and leaned closer to me, "I came to warn you, my love. Tread carefully, as those closest to you shall be your demise. Now I shall leave you with a parting gift."

Once again kissing me, she suddenly bit my lips, "Take with you the last of my essence. Whoever you kiss after this kiss shall devote herself to you completely, but only once shall this work, so choose your soul mate wisely, my love, for you shall need it for the upcoming battle."

As she stood, before me I saw her slowly fade. Letting me go she walked back, "I once loved a man, and he stole my heart. Gain it back, and all the power he sought shall be yours, my love."

I stood in confusion. As she faded, I said, "Wait, what are you talking about?" But before I could finish talking she had faded completely.

Holding my throat I stood still for a second, "That demon, but how?" Taking a deep breath I got dressed, and made my way to my room, only to find Adriel was gone. He had left before we could talk, but had left a letter.

"Orion, this life is a cruel life. I've seen so many perish, so many die, and yet nothing changes. The endless cycle took those I loved. It has taken everything from me, and now I look at you and I can see that you're going to change this kingdom somehow. I'm not sure how but you will, and when you do I want to be the sword that you use to change it. I saw this in my dreams. I saw that you stood in a battlefield, victorious, but there was something that worries me, my friend. The dream ends with another man sitting upon a burning throne, as the ashes of everything fall around him. I could not see who this man was, but I hope this was not a vision of our future, as if so it shall end in ash. My father came from a long bloodline of ancient people called the watchers, men who could envision events from the future. Enough about all the chaos, I only wish to tell you that I believe in your dream, and I wish to thank you for being a good friend and more so like a brother to me. Even with all the silence between us all here, I can see how we all care for one another."

The letter ended, and I sat in my bed, overwhelmed by everything. I felt as if from the moment I desired to be king my life had fallen down a path I could not control. But somehow I was able to take it all in and keep going. Maybe it was the thought of one day being the king I desired to be that allowed me to live through all of this, allowing me to keep my sanity in this insane world.

The following day I made my way to the west with Adriel, Visan, and a newcomer who barely spoke. After Blake had taken the throne he began to expedite the training of knights, merely to gain numbers rather than quality soldiers. The boy who I had never seen seemed afraid and even unable to properly put his armor on. I could tell the lack of training he had had.

In an attempt to befriend the boy I asked, "Hey, my name's Orion. Tell me, what's your name?"

"Ziek. I've heard a lot about you. They say you and your master are traitors, but I don't believe a word of it. Sir Nigh once helped my family when we were being harassed by a group of drunken men. Ever since then, we've been ever so grateful. I know he's an honorable man."

"Thanks, I'm glad you're on our side. So, what's your talent? Most knights are known to have better trades than others. For example I can dual wield really good while Visan is rather quick with any kind of blade, large or small."

"Sorry, I've got none. We graduated too quickly."

"I see, well we should be on our way. It's good to have met you."

"Same here."

Walking closer to me Adriel asked me to not speak about the letter, that we would talk once the mission was over, and so we kept our minds on the task at hand. Before leaving the kingdom I saw the people with fear in their faces. King Blake had brought his own men and they had brought new laws to the kingdom. This was no longer the same kingdom I had grown to love. The people quietly looked down around the knights and never smiled. Except one, Smith, who smiled as he stood up and waved at me while we were leaving. But when he did, one of the knights came over and began to scream at him. When the knight did that I moved back to where they were, but before I could get there Vivian stood in front of me.

"Orion, don't even think about it. Let's go."

"Vivian? That man is my friend. I can't let them treat him like that."

"Orion, right now you're lucky to be alive. Be happy that you still have your hands and legs. He'll be fine, so let's go."

Vivian escorted us out to the west, and informed us that she would be back soon with some information. We would just keep our guard up for any enemies. While riding towards the guard posts Vivian informed us of our mission. "Ok, listen up. We ride to the western point, where you all will keep each other safe and remain vigilant for enemy presence. Adriel, you will be in charge. I need someone with a level head who's not too keen on their emotions. While in this post, one will patrol around the area, always keeping an eye on the tower, while the others stay in the tower. You all have had excellent training, so I can only see success. Am I right?"

We all agreed. When we finally reached the post, Vivian helped us set up our areas, and then pulled me aside. "Orion, stay calm and be patient. There are things your master and I have been investigating."

"Vivian, how can I stay calm when I can see before my very eyes the cruelty that king has brought? No great leader should punish those beneath him like he has done. People do not wish to follow a man like him."

"Orion, I see that, but for now we have our hands tied. Keep your mind sane. You're a great hope for Nigh and I. We've seen you grow to be a fine young man. I can remember when you were but a boy, and now look at you, a grown man. You must be nearing adulthood. I can already see hair growing on your face. You have become more than a student for Nigh. I hope you know he sees you as a son. It's rather sweet to see a man such as Nigh feel so deeply for another. That's why I know you're amazing. I'll spend the night here, since it's getting dark already and it wouldn't be safe to ride back alone."

That night we all gathered around a fire, eating and telling jokes. It made me feel a bit at ease. I could also see the others needed some time to relax. After moments of sitting together, Visan climbed the tower while Ziek walked off with Adriel.

Vivian and I stayed by the fire. Looking at her I noticed how her eyes lit up each time she spoke of Nigh. "Say Vivian, do you and my master have something?"

"Orion? What a question. Well it's complicated. He and I have never been the lover type, but after many years of battle we all find that bit of joy. Nigh is a man with a grand heart, even if he wishes to not admit it. I've seen him love, and there's no other flame as bright as that one."

"Really? I didn't know you and him had something so deep."

"It's not I who he loves, but that's a story for another day. We should rest now, as I must ride at first light."

"I see. Sorry I asked such a deep question."

"No worries."

Vivian stood up, holding her abdomen, as she smiled. While looking up she turned to me. "One day when you fall in love, keep her by your side. Love can be the most powerful thing."

"Or the most painful."

"All great things come at a price."

Walking off, I could only think of everything we had endured throughout all these years, "Life really weighs heavy on the mind. I'm so young, yet I feel so old."

But before she entered her tent Vivian looked at me. "Please, keep yourself under control. I shall be back soon after I leave tomorrow, and we'll see what's truly going on here."

Waking up the next day I noticed Vivian had left. Standing by her tent I couldn't help but think of the situation back at the kingdom. The new king, Blake, had changed our kingdom. No longer did I see men of honor but rather slaves. The knights had been scattered and Nigh, the leader, had been disbanded from the knights along with Oberon and Zangar. I'd been sent to the western outskirts of the kingdom to protect after the group of the Blood Hand had sent out threats against the king. But for what? The kingdom had already fallen. Maybe the Blood Hand should make its way over there and kill that king.

Visan and Adriel joined me at the post, but even they had changed. Visan seemed lost in thought more often than not, and I, too, had little time these days to share words with either of them. Adriel seemed a bit more lively than us both, with his constant upbeat attitude. But I feared there was more here than what we saw. Why had the knights been disbanded? And why had we been sent so far from the kingdom?

Ziek was rather lonesome and I had not the mind to speak many words with him, since there was so much more happening here.

Days passed, and there was no sign from Vivian, but we continued to wait for further words from her or anyone.

One morning, while looking down from the tower, I noticed that

Visan waved. "Hey Orion, let's change posts. I'm tired of being down here. I'd like some fresh air up there."

"Ok, I need to rest either way."

Making my way down I grabbed my sword and went to the inner area where we had set up camp, while Visan took over the tower watch. This post was exposed and lonely. I had no idea why we had been left here for over two weeks. Although, I knew one thing for sure, there was something wrong, but what could we do? If we didn't follow orders we would no longer be knights like our masters.

The day passed as many other days and nights came to us like the wind. I could feel the cold breeze flow through the trees as the howl of the wind reached my ears. I lost myself in the idea of Aleya being here at my side.

"Orion, where are the others?" said a soft voice. Looking back I saw Vivian with Anibel riding closer to us.

"Vivian, it's been a long time. What brings you all the way out here?"

"Gather the others. We must talk."

"On my way."

Moving quickly I ran out to gather the others. Adriel was eating with one of the new recruits as Visan stood atop the tower, by himself.

"Hey Adriel, Visan, go back to the camp," I yelled.

Visan asked, "Why? I'm on watch."

"Vivian is here, so let's go."

We all quickly gathered around as Vivian sat with us. She held a map of the area and began to explain, "We've gathered intel on those calling themselves the Blood Hand. They're being led by a man who we believe to be Alastor, an assassin who once bested even Nigh in combat. Now here's where we are." She pointed to our location on the map. We stood far to the western area, near a river.

Vivian had a sharp look in her eyes, "And the enemy has been using this river to transport equipment. We believe they'll try to attack the city, so we must take the camp down and make our way further in. We can't risk being seen, but we must also try and gather further intel from a fort they're using. We can make our way to the northern area and try to stay hidden within the trees, but the goal will be to see what they're planning. I'll be here with you and have called for reinforcement, which should be here in a few hours. Gather your things. We'll move now."

I looked closer at the map. "Wait, but if we move too far north, they may not be there. Wouldn't they want to be closer to the south, to move quicker?"

Vivian smiled, "Yes, this is true. Very perceptive, Orion, but we will move far north to come down from there, allowing us to move down the river while we still maintain our position hidden. If not, we risk running into them, since we're not aware of their exact position."

"I see, so what exactly will we do?"

"What we will look for is their capabilities. I want numbers, equipment, and details of the leader. He's the priority. We've been hunting this man for many years. Nigh is the only man to have faced the assassin in combat and to survive. If he's there, we won't engage in any way. The man is far too skilled for any of us to manage. I saw him take down an entire squad of abyss knights on his own."

"Wait, isn't Master in charge of the abyssal knights?"

"Yes, he and Logan were the ones in charge of our special units. Nigh led the Abyssal knights and Logan the Crimson knights."

Adriel walked closer, "Sir. Vivian, I can feel someone watching us."

We all looked around, as Vivian pulled out her two daggers, "What do you mean? From where?"

Looking around I could not see anything, but suddenly a man dressed in black rushed from behind Vivian. Turning around she quickly moved back. He pulled out his sword with lightning speed, moved in front of Vivian and stabbed her multiple times. His speed was inhuman, his movements blurred my vision, and my body fell into paralysis. Vivian fell to the ground while holding her abdomen as she coughed out blood. She cried out, "Noooooo!" Her hands twitched, and tears came out of her eyes. She looked at the man with anger, throwing a knife at his throat. She mortally wounded him. But from the shadows came a second man. We all gathered around him. All we could see were his piercing dark eyes, as cloth covered his face.

"Such a pity, I didn't expect this to end so quickly," said the assassin.

Adriel walked forward, without fear, while the rest of us quivered.

Looking back at us he said, "Now who said it was over, assassin? Orion, Visan, new guy, leave this place. I'll take care of this one."

All I could think about was how much I wanted to run, "Adriel, what are you doing? He killed Vivian."

"She isn't dead yet, but you mustn't worry about her. I'll see to her wounds. She'll slow you guys down. You must go and get reinforcements."

Running towards the man, they both moved with tremendous speed. I'd never seen Adriel fight this way. Watching them clash made me feel helpless and powerless. I, the one who always said would be the one to save them, stood there powerless.

The assassin asked Adriel, "Who are you boy? You're worthy of death at my hands."

Smiling, Adriel said, "My name's Adriel, second son of Alastor."

"Alastor, you say. Why, that's the name my master took when he killed that devil of a knight. To think I get the chance to meet his son. Oh, the irony."

This man said that he was not Alastor? I believed with the level of skill he possessed he would be the one Vivian had warned us about. If this assassin is this powerful then what hope would we have to fight against Alastor? This man was as skilled as the one who had wounded Vivian in two moves, yet him and Adriel were evenly matched. And Adriel never said a word about his father.

Adriel moved back, "Go now, you guys need to warn the south."

Turning around we all ran. As I looked back I told Adriel, "We'll come back, just hang in there." As we kept running I saw another man step forward, but this man had his face revealed, and he had short black hair, and dark eyes, with olive skin, and a scar across his face. *Could that be, Alastor?* I saw him look at us with a smile, as he vanished back into the forest.

Looking forward again, I screamed, "Look out." But before the words reached them he appeared in front of us, stabbing the new recruit multiple times. The kid screamed as he stabbed him. The assassin placed his hand on his mouth, while lifting his lifeless body with the daggers deep inside him, and tossing the body to the side.

"You must be Orion. Tell me, where is your master?"

Moving back I said, "To hell with you."

Visan stood in front of me. "Orion, we've never been the best of friends nor have we spoken, but the truth is, I've always admired you. Let me distract him, and then please run."

But when he finished telling me this with a smile, the assassin had already reached him, stabbing him in the side and then pushing him aside.

"Such passionate words from this one. I want you, Orion, to watch as he bleeds to death."

How did this man know my name? Was this the end for me? Would I die here? I began to tremble so much that I fell to my knees. This man had such great power and a promise of death beyond any I had ever seen. I didn't want to die. I could feel tears in my eyes."

"Are you begging for your life? I'd expect more honor from Nigh's pupil. How sad! I suppose you can't hope for much fight these days. Now die!" he yelled as he ran towards me.

I held my breath as he rushed towards me. Closing my eyes, I could see nothing but darkness as I felt his dagger pierce through me. I felt my body go into shock, and as I opened my eyes, I saw the man with a smile staring at me.

"Tell me, Orion, how does death taste? How does it feel to drown in your own blood? But before you die, I'll tell you a secret. The one who sits upon your throne ordered us to come here. I'd say the cruelty." He laughed.

I felt myself drowning in my own blood, as I gasped for air, but as I tried to breathe everything went blurry. Coughing out blood I slowly closed my eyes. I could see nothing, but darkness, and then I heard a voice call to me, "My king, set me free. Let me end this suffering."

Opening my eyes I looked at the assassin, as he stared at me with strange eyes. Looking down I saw my body covered in black armor, as black smoke poured out from my chest where the assassin had his hand. Slowly the assassin's hand was pushed back as the world around me turned black and white. I saw what looked like a black gauntlet push his dagger out from inside me. As the hand continued to push the dagger I noticed the hole in my chest slowly close around the gauntlet, and then the hand continued to move out from within me, pushing the assassin far back with tremendous force. I could not believe what I was seeing. I then felt my chest breaking and with unbearable pain I screamed, but I faintly saw what looked like a knight break free from within me. Falling back I saw my body had been opened up from the inside out. I saw my organs, my heart beating, as it slowly closed itself. The pain slowly left me, as anger replaced it.

"Now this is more like you. I was wondering where your creature was hiding."

The black knight stood before me, wearing the same armor that I had just moments ago. Looking back at me I saw a dark aura enveloped around him. It was the same as before; the shadow that had always been around me. Extending his hand an enormous sword grew from his hand.

"Mortal, you wound the king of this world, and for that I shall paint the land red with your blood," said the knight with a deep sinister voice. It made my skin crawl as it sounded like a true demon.

"It may not be so easy, creature. I don't plan on dying here."

Without a word the knight rushed in but the assassin moved away quickly, only to bump into another knight. As he grabbed the assassin by the throat, the assassin stretched out his hand with what looked like a stone as he smiled, "Take this, you fiend." But the knight grabbed his hand and crushed it along with the assassin's stone. Screaming in pain the assassin said, "Impossible. He said that would kill you."

"Man possesses no threat to me, merely grains of sand for me to step upon."

The second knight walked closer to the assassin and with force cut both of his legs off, while the other knight tossed him to the side. The assassin crawled towards me with a smile, "What in hell's name are you, child? What is this creature?"

The knight followed him as the second knight turned to a black mist and fused with him. "Crawl, beg for your life, human. Look from the ground upon the face of your king, before I take your head."

I watched in shock, but I could see this knight held me as king, and he was more powerful than anything I had ever seen. But I had a better idea. "Wait, don't kill him. I'd rather he live without his legs, so he lives with the torment of never being able to kill again. Now assassin, tell me how you know my name? And you said you knew this knight? How do you know these things?"

Laughing, the assassin said, "You really are oblivious to the ways of the world, are you not? Well, Alastor did want you to know the truth in the end. So I'll tell you, kid. A few years ago, a man came to the Blood Hand and asked for our help. He gave us gold and asked us to overthrow the kingdom of the south. In the midst of the chaos he asked a small group of us to kill the villagers around the south as he said that they would be in the way of his plans. So we did. I was there the night they went to your village. But were we in for a surprise, as you did the job for us. Oh, you should have seen what you did."

His words made me angry, "What the hell do you mean? You were there? That's a lie. There were no survivors, and what do you mean I did the job for you?" I walked closer to the assassin and grabbed him by the throat.

"You lie," I shouted.

"Look kid, I'm about to die. I don't care if you believe me, but the truth is that when me and my men killed your old man, you lost it. From nowhere that damned black knight came and started to kill my men, but for some reason while I was standing still in shock you walked past me and ordered the knight to kill the villagers as well. It was a blood bath, kid. You were death in flesh. I'd never seen someone so thirsty for vengeance. What surprised me the most is how you killed that boy who begged for his life. He kneeled in front of you and begged you to spare him. But you had your demon cut the boy in two. I was in disbelief. I knew if I ran I'd die, so I waited my turn. But ironically you held a knife to my face and cut me, resulting in this scar you see here. You told me to run and never forget you. Trust me, not a day goes by when I don't think of that night. You truly are a monster. I've never met someone so ruthless."

"You call me a monster. You're the one who kills for no reason."

"I kill for gold, boy. You killed for the sheer joy. You should have seen your face, with the eyes of a killer. You truly think that you're good, but tell me what good is there in all the death you bring?"

Grabbing my knife I cut his throat, "The good of your silence!"

The man coughed out blood as he choked, "You monster! But know this, we aren't to blame. The one who ordered us is your king. Blake is the reason we were there in the first place, and he is the one who has ordered us to dispose of you and the others now."

The man slowly closed his eyes, "King Blake? What the hell do you mean?"

But without a response he laid on my hands, lifeless. His words brought anger to me, but I knew that there must have been some truth in them. I knew I could not have been the one to have killed my own people. Looking at the knight I asked him, "Knight, was what this man said true?"

Turning around the knight said, "The swine speaks the truth" then he vanished and I was left in shock. I had been the one who had killed all those from my village. It had been me all along. I was the reason they had all died. But, no wait, none of this would have happened if Blake hadn't sent those assassins to the village. It was him. He's the reason why all of this had happened. I wouldn't forgive him.

I heard footsteps approaching me, and looking back I saw Adriel standing in shock. "Orion, is all of this true? Did you kill your own people?"

"Adriel, I can explain."

"No, what the hell is that thing that was just here? That wasn't human!"

"He's a knight, and he came here to help us. It's not what you think."

"Orion, nothing good can come from this. That thing is a demon."

Standing up I told him, "Adriel, you heard the same as what I heard. The king has betrayed his people. That man is the reason why all of this is happening, and you stand here accusing me of wrongs. If the knight that helps me is a demon then I'd rather that demon be by my side than a backstabbing man with a crown."

Walking away Adriel said, "You're no knight. You're no better than the assassin."

Screaming at him I said, "Why? I'm doing my duty for my people."

"You think you can save your people by stepping into the darkness like that? Have you not learned from the past that those who use the dark arts are damned, while those seeking revenge just trigger a vicious cycle?"

"If that's so then I shall be damned for eternity because I won't stand by and watch King Blake murder more innocent people, Adriel. If you wish you can stand with me or against me. I won't beg you to understand."

"So what if I stand against you, Orion?"

Walking forward I said, "You'll do no such thing, Adriel."

"You'll have to kill me, Orion, if you want to silence me."

Taking a deep breath I said, "No, I'll create a new world for you to see, and one day you'll understand."

Stepping back Adriel smiled, "We shall see, next time we meet."

Turning around and walking into the darkness, he slowly disappeared.

"Orion, hey."

I heard Nigh's voice in the distance. As I could see torches coming closer I made my way back to where Vivian's body was. *How do I explain all this to Nigh?* I saw Vivian still alive, gasping for air. Adriel had attended to her wounds but then had left after our conversation. Vivian would not make it much longer. She looked at me. "Orion, you have a gift, I can see it. Nigh really cares for you. I hope you know that."

"Don't speak, save your strength. You're badly injured."

Finally reaching me Nigh slowly walked to where Vivian laid, his eyes open wide with pain as his hands trembled, "Orion, what happened here? Who did this?"

Feeling Nigh's pain I didn't know how to respond as Nigh fell to his knees holding her close to him. "Vivian, who did this to you?"

Looking up at Nigh, she smiled. "Nigh, you promised me you'd never cry if this happened to me, so don't you dare cry now."

"But…"

"Shhh, it has been a long life, but I must tell you that the south has betrayed you."

"What?"

Vivan started to breathe heavily as she extended her hand to her stomach. Placing Nigh's hand on her stomach she then reached Nigh's face. "I was finally able to taste the love of your lips. Do you feel that, my love? Life grows inside me." She slowly moved closer to Nigh and kissed him as he just looked at her, with tears in his eyes. Her hand quickly dropped as she lay in his arms, lifeless.

"A life? Vivian? No, ahhhhhhh!! No, not like this. I'll kill them. I'll kill them all."

I saw Nigh looking at his hands as he saw the blood that had come from Vivian's stomach. "A life? There's no life in this world."

As Nigh's anger grew, I felt the air become denser. The wind began to howl and rain slowly began to drizzle, as if the world felt his endless pain.

Oberon put his hand on my shoulder, "Orion, tell us what happened? Who did this to Vivian?"

With a sigh I said, "The king ordered the assassins to come here."

Quickly turning his face towards me I saw the rage in his eyes, "The king? The assassins? You mean they did this?"

Looking away I said, "Yes."

Nigh placed her body back down on the floor. "I see the king shall pay. However, the Blood Hand still has men in this forest?"

"I believe so, Master, but they're beyond skilled, so we should leave this place."

Walking towards the forest Nigh looked at me, "No, this ends tonight. They shall all die. This I swear."

Oberon and Zangar both looked at each other, and Oberon said, "We'll follow you to the end, Nigh."

Nigh climbed his horse, "Orion go back, this is too dangerous."

"But Master, I can't just go back. They also killed Vivian, and hurt both Visan and Adriel."

Nigh turned towards the forest, "Orion, take Visan to a safe place."

Oberon looked at Nigh. "Nigh, I'll take Visan, and Vivian's body. I'm the only skilled medic here, so I'll attend to his wounds. Let the boy go in my stead. It's time he grew to become a true knight, even if it must be a bloody path, he must one day witness the madness of war."

Nigh agreed and asked me to get ready to ride to where the assassins were.

Climbing on one of the horses I said, "I'll stay alive."

Riding down the forest line we were barely able to keep up with Nigh as he rode furiously. I looked at Zangar and asked, "Does he know where he's going?"

Zangar looked at me and said, "Yes, we found out where their hideout is. They're staying at an old fort once used by us, but after the last war it was completely destroyed, so we abandoned it."

"A fort? But how will four of us raid a fort?"

Looking at Nigh he said, "Orion, tonight you'll see why Nigh gained the title of Abyss walker in the war against the Blood Hand."

Looking at Nigh I felt anger unlike any I had ever felt from him, and I saw cinder slowly light up, as if ready to burn everything to ashes.

Nigh looked back at us. "The fort is just a little further. I shall take the gate, and you all come after I break through."

After moments we reached an old fort. It looked torn apart but still had high walls and a large wooden gate. Nigh climbed down from his horse and walked forward and grabbing cinder in his right hand, he looked back at us. "Stand back."

As soon as Nigh stepped off his horse two men rushed at him from the wood line, too fast for me to even see clearly. But Nigh had already noticed and had prepared what looked like a bomb. Stepping close to the one from the left, Nigh allowed the man to pierce his abdomen, so he could be close enough. Grabbing the man's throat, Nigh forced the bomb into the man's mouth, tossing him towards the other man. He then grabbed cinder using its flame to ignite the bomb, blowing the two men to pieces.

Everything happened so fast that I could not believe he could calculate all this with such precision. Looking at Zangar I asked, "I thought those were forbidden, only used by those from the north?"

"They are, but he is allowed to use whatever means necessary to accomplish the mission, since he has to burden the death of thousands so that the rest can live in peace. You see, Nigh was eventually trained to take the place of the old Abyssal Knight, and there could only be one, because like the title they're turned to beasts of the void, men capable of what you see here."

"Are you two going to just stand there?"

Zangar laughed. "I'm making sure your little pet knows how crazy you are!"

"Let's go. Now isn't the time for jokes."

As Nigh held cinder in his hands we noticed screams coming from within the fort. Nigh looked at us, confused, as he slowly walked forward. I could faintly see what looked like corpses at the front of the gate. They had been impaled by spears, as their bodies dangled in the air. The three of us moved closer. As we walked by the bodies we saw countless ones which had been torn apart. Nigh said, "What in creation's name is this? Someone killed the assassins before we could even get here."

Walking inside the gate we heard crunching as if something was being bitten. Looking far into the distance stood Logan as he bit into the heart of a man. We all stood in place, as Nigh pointed his sword at Logan. "What the hell are you doing here?"

Logan tossed the body. "Long time no see, Nigh." As he said his last word he appeared in front of Nigh grabbing his sword with his bare hands. "Break."

With one word Nigh's sword shattered into pieces. A sword known to be an old relic had just been destroyed by his mere hands. Nigh dropped the sword and pulled out a dagger, stabbing Logan. Then dropping another bomb, while moving back, he quickly grabbed one of the shattered pieces of the sword and threw it at the bomb, igniting it. The explosion was tremendous, as it pushed debris all over.

But as the smoke cleared up Logan stood with a smile and grabbed Nigh by the neck. "I've always wondered what your blood tastes like. No worries, I merely wish to have a taste." Biting into Nigh, Logan's eyes turned black, as he pulled back and dropped Nigh. "It was you."

Holding his neck Nigh walked to the side. It seemed as if he was badly hurt from the bite. Zangar pulled out his blade. "Now you are mine," he yelled as he rushed at Logan, cutting into Logan's shoulder from behind.

Falling to his knees, Logan held the sword. "Mortals, always fighting the inevitable."

Nigh walked closer to Logan, "You'll die for everything you've done. I don't care what the hell you are, or why you are doing all of this."

Standing up from his knees, Logan pulled the blade away from his shoulder, as his body healed and then his crimson armor repaired before our very eyes. "Nigh, you can't kill a man who no longer lives."

"We will see."

Zangar suddenly ran towards Logan. "You two talk too much," he said as he landed a strong blow on Logan's face. However, when I looked closer I realized Logan held his arm and Zangar still hadn't noticed that Logan had cut it off. With a look of surprise Zangar stepped back, his eyes fueled with rage. "What the hell, my arm."

Logan tossed Zangar's arm and slowly walked closer. "Like I said, nothing you can do."

Logan rushed Nigh, once again holding him but this time as he held him, his skin turned as black as the night, slamming Nigh into the wall. Logan's force was so great that the wall crumbled with Nigh inside.

Stepping away from the rubble Logan's skin once again turned white as he walked closer to me.

"Call him, call Nis."

Quivering in fear I moved back and as I did so the knight appeared before me once again. I suddenly felt relief. But Logan smiled with a cynical smile. "Well now, it seems you've yet to make the pact so you need motivation. Orion, you have yet to see the truths of the kingdoms."

The knight created a sword and rushed Logan, but Logan extended his arm, paralyzing the knight in his tracks. "You surely don't believe that Nis can stop me as he is now, Orion? Vanish!" With the words vanish symbols appeared around Logan and the knight turned into smoke and was gone.

Looking around in desperation I noticed that Nigh was unconscious and Zangar laid on the floor bleeding. Logan looked at them and then at me, "Orion, I haven't come here to kill any of you, I've come here to warn you that there's a great war to come."

Logan walked close to Zangar and placed his hand above the wound, closing it. As he did it looked like he had suddenly aged and then came back to normal again. Looking back at me he said, "There, he shall live, but you must come with me. There's much we have to discuss."

"I'll never go with you!" I screamed.

Logan looked at me with anger, "You have no choice." Rushing me, he grabbed my throat. "Now sleep," and all went dark.

I could faintly hear him as I drifted into darkness "The time has come for you to reign as king of all lands."

# CHAPTER 7

## THE CROWNLESS KING

*The year is 1118*

*Where am I?* I asked myself.

"You are in paradise," said a deep, familiar voice, but I could see nothing in the darkness. Taking a few steps forward, my eyes slowly adjusted, and slowly I saw what looked like a throne. On the back of the throne there were three skeletons with their hands raised in the air as if praising something, while the rest of the throne was made of skeleton parts, and where the hands rested there were skulls. Upon the throne sat a dark entity; a figure in the shape of a boy.

Standing from the throne, the dark figure stepped forth. Each step echoed, as it said, "Tarnished by the feet of man this kingdom shall not be." The voice changed from a deep voice to a young boy's voice. The young boy's voice sounded familiar, but it was faint and I could not hear it exactly, as it also sounded like there were a hundred other voices behind that voice.

"Where am I?" I asked with fear in my chest.

"Allow me to show you the truth of man."

Looking around I could not explain what stood before me, but the closer I looked the more I could see what looked like the night sky within the darkness of this being.

"What are you?"

"I am that which peers into thou soul. Now watch, seeker of kingship."

Everything around me turned into what looked like mirrors. I witnessed men killing each other. Some seemed to pray before battle, as they readied their blades in the name of their god. Thousands, bearing the insignia of the south marched into battle as they shouted, "In the name of creation." Rushing down the field, the men met against another, smaller legion, who wore no armor, and looked more like peasants than knights. With death in their eyes the men ravished the lands of their foes. It mattered not whom it was; men, women, and children all fell to the name of their truth. In one instant a knight came across a young boy who had survived the onslaught. The boy crawled out of his burning home, only to find that his mom lay scorched before him. Crying, the boy held his mother's hand. The knight stood in place, watching with pity, turning around as if to ignore what he had seen. The knights intended to allow the boy to live. Walking away the knight was soon met with another knight, one wearing heavy armor, who looked like the leader. Ordering the knight to go back and slay the kid, the leader pointed at the child, as he said, "That boy is an abomination. He must die. He is one of them. Now take up your sword and kill that beast." Refusing to kill the child the knight was struck down by the leader, falling to the floor. The knight watched as they beheaded the kid in front of him. The leader called for his men, ordering them to bring a rope, stating that the knight had betrayed them and should be punished with death. Soon after the knight was stripped from all positions and hung from a tree. The men stood around watching his life drift away, but none moved to aid the dying knight, as the leader had branded him a traitor. The mirror soon fogged and another began to show images, showing a group of men sitting in a darkened room plotting to kill an unknown king in order to gain power. But as they all sat in place, each ones thoughts became clear. I could hear their inner voices planning to kill one another after they no longer needed each other's aid. The mirror soon faded, showing all the men dead, as only one stood, and another man stood within the shadows whose eyes glowed a deep red. Hollowing, the mirror showed nothing. Looking to my side I could see another mirror as it began to display images. Men holding bags of gold while leaving a kingdom in ruin, smiling while holding the gold bloodied by those they had murdered. Behind them I could see the corpses of what looked like a family. The man had been stabbed as the woman and child had been burned. Without a care in the world the men spoke of their riches and how the woman had been good entertainment. These images angered me and made me wish men like those would all just die, as I could see the cruelty of war, the greed of man, and the wrath of their desires. The outcome of each war was merely chaos, none had meaning or purpose, men just sought their own empowerment through the sacrifice of others. To think that women were taken and raped right before their throats were slit. Children were hung, and men tore to pieces. I had witnessed hundreds of bodies burn as soldiers marched into battles.

"Do you see, this is the world you humans have created? This is what your kind knows. This is your destiny. Endless chaos, endless death, all in the name of honor, love, faith, or whatever your kind can find just. The world seeks balance. Within the blood, within the cries of thousands, one must rise, for the time of cleansing shall come."

"Time of cleansing? What do you mean?"

"All life has a balance it must follow, but humans have upset this balance with your wicked ways. I've watched you kill each other for far too long, thus the lands you so desperately protect shall wither and decay. They shall seize to exist, as the chaos fuels the end. The chaos is fueled by the death and despair of humanity. In time all that once held a form shall soon turn to nothing. Only one such as you can end this by uniting humanity. If humanity doesn't unite under the dream of the true king, all shall wither and die before your very eyes."

"A true king?"

"A truth has been spoken, human."

"How would I be able to rule if I have nothing?"

"You have been given a guardian, once a mortal, but now a shadow of his former self. This guardian is the key given to sit upon the throne of man."

"Do you mean the knight of black armor?"

"Yes, his armor mirrors your heart, however you have yet to seal the pact with the guardian."

The knight in black armor stepped forward as he bowed before me.

"King of kings."

"Who are you? This thing says you were once a mortal. Tell me who were you before?"

"We are a thousand soulless knights."

"A thousand soulless knights? Do you remember your name?"

"No, we are many, not one."

Looking back at the dark entity I asked, "What does he mean?"

"Before you kneel to Nis, the soulless knight, bearer of a thousand souls, each soul within him is a life he has taken, each life its own struggle, yet Nis has no soul of his own. He is merely a vessel, created for the sin of man."

"Created for the sin of man?"

"Indeed. In such a sinful world where would all the evil exist, if not within a vessel?"

"But Nis is my protector. How can the vessel that holds all of man's sins be the one to protect me, and guide me to the throne of man?"

"Only a sinner can exalt man of his sins."

"If what you say is true then what becomes of me?"

"Each pact formed with Nis grants you more power, the power needed to rule, the power to save them all. However, each pact breaks a seal within Nis. There are four seals, one for each sin that controls thou lands: lust, pride, envy, and wrath. Each sin is present in the creation of the wars waged. Each sin has taken a hold of the lands and its people. Once broken, the seals may never be undone. The choice is yours, Orion. Shall you sacrifice your humanity for the power needed to be king? Or shall you watch as the world burns before your very eyes?"

"You say it as if it'd be easy to do either, but tell me, how do I release a seal?"

"You shall know when the time comes, and the pact shall be made."

"What if I refuse?"

"Then all shall perish."

After his words I suddenly woke up, startled. Looking around I could see that I had been chained to a bed. "Where am I?"

Walking in I saw Straif, Logan's apprentice, step inside with water and food, "You're in the Nikostratos camp."

"The Nikostratos camp?"

"Yes, this is the victory army. Master Logan gathered men from all across the lands to fight for our noble cause."

"What do you want? Why don't you just kill me now?"

"Orion, don't be so foolish. I have no desire to kill you. Master Logan brought you here so that we can work together."

"What are you talking about? Your master is a murderer. He killed the crimson knights and it's because of him that the south was lost to King Blake."

With anger Straif said, "Is that what you think? Orion, he could have killed every single person in that kingdom had he so desired."

"Well then what stopped him?"

"You did. When he spoke to you he said he saw there was yet hope for humanity. You have no idea what Master Logan has had to endure for his people. Every life he takes he must endure their sorrow, and he isn't one to take life for granted. It was your king, your kingdom, and these wretched lands that drove him to do what he did. I've seen him spend countless hours trying to plan how to help those in need."

"You think I'm going to believe you? After seeing him take the lives of so many then attempting to kill my master and Zangar, all I believe is that he's a monster, not even human."

"The same could be said of that knight who protects you. You and I both know it was you who murdered all those people when you were a child. Yet you wish to sit here and sound innocent. You wish to justify what you have done with words instead of actions. All the blood you have spilled and yet you say that Logan is evil? Well you should take a look at yourself before you dare raise a finger to point at others. The man has spent countless amount of time attempting to fix these lands. There is far more evil out there, Orion. No man is innocent in this life, we all do wrong, but it is who does the wrong for the good who in truth is worthy. Master Logan may have murdered those of the crimson knights, but they had been working for Blake. The men were evil and needed to be dealt with. He told me that when you saw him, you looked at him with hate. He wished it would not have been you because he believes in you."

Straif's words took me by surprise. Maybe Logan and I weren't so different after all. Maybe there was more to this than I knew. "So tell me, where's Logan now?"

"He left. He has left the rest to you. He said he was going to find the one they call the Father of Alchemy."

"The Father of Alchemy?"

"Yes, the one who brought alchemy to this land."

"So that man is real?"

"Very much so."

"What does he want to see him for?"

"He hasn't told me, but as we have much to do ourselves, we need not worry about what he is doing."

"Wait, I've yet to agree to even help you. I don't even know what happened to Nigh, Zangar, Oberon, Adriel, and Visan."

"They were captured by the south, and they're currently being held in the prison there."

"What? Why didn't Logan take them somewhere too?"

"Orion, you keep living in this dream world. Wake up and realize that there's never a perfect ending to all things."

"I know, but now they're being held in the south at the mercy of King Blake, a man who's willing to do what it takes to make an example of those who oppose him."

"Yes, that will happen, but not if we act quickly."

"What do you mean?"

"We have raised an army to bring down King Blake and his tyranny."

"And you want me to join this army of yours I presume?"

"We want you to lead the army."

"You want me to lead your army when I have yet to even see combat? Are you mad?"

"You don't need to worry about that. I'll help you reach into the depths of yourself. You'll learn how to harness the power of that which protects you and we'll use that to gain the upper hand."

"How?"

"Master Logan left me instructions and all his tools to help you gain what you need. He said to warn you that it will hurt a bit and you have to have your heart completely set on doing this in order for it to work."

What Straif spoke of was the power of Nis, of this I am sure, but I had seen in my dream that for reaching deeper into the power I'd slowly lose my humanity. I still had no idea what would become of me if I were to break the seals. "This is way too much to think about right now. So many things have happened that I can't just agree to this."

"Well, you must decide quickly, for the life of your master, and all others across the land hangs in the balance."

I could see that he was attempting to pressure me into deciding hastily, but, what if he was right? If Nigh was in the south it would only be a matter of time before they executed him and the others as well. It seemed I had little choice here. If I didn't decide now I would once again allow those around me to die, just like my father, Leon, and Vivian. They had all perished because I was unable to act, and I couldn't keep running from this.

"Ok, teach me what I have to do, and then I can decide. I can't just throw myself into this plan of yours, but I'll see what you have to show me."

"First, let's go. You should meet those who shall follow you."

Stepping outside I could see hundreds of people walking around. Some were crafting armor, others forging swords, and some were training in the back with swords, axes, and arrows.

"So we are mercenaries?" I asked.

"Well we have no kingdom, so you can say we are freedom fighters. That sounds better than mercenaries I'd say."

"To think that Logan had been planning this is absurd. Where are we? I mean, this camp is enormous. Where could he have hidden such an army?"

"We're in the north, in the kingdom of Bartholomaios."

"What? But these lands are cursed?"

"That's just a tale to scare children, Orion. This place isn't cursed. It has many legends but there's no such curse that holds this land. Logan chose this place because no one would ever think to come here, exactly because of that."

"I have a question. What happened to King Alantt?"

"No one knows. Logan was also confused as to where he went off to. He believes the king set sail to the old lands across the sea to the east."

"Really? Why would he think that?"

"Because that was where the first king set his kingdom and there's something there that holds great power, but I'm not sure. Maybe when you see Logan you can ask him. I do know that King Alantt had many secrets that Logan was looking for, which pointed to the Kingdom of Old."

"I see, well I'll ask him."

"Walk around, Orion. Get to know the people."

"So you don't want to keep an eye on me? What makes you think I won't run off?"

"Like I said, the only way you can do this is if you desire it in your heart. Now that you know the truth we have no need to keep you in chains. Now you make the choice. But I have to get back to prepare some things. Later we shall ride down near the eastern kingdom, close to the southern border so that you may see a few things."

Straif walked away. As I went back inside the tent, I sat there thinking to myself. *I have to try and make sense of all of this. That dream I had must mean something. Maybe Straif can help me figure this all out. I do need Logan and what he knows in order to help Nigh, but will I be siding with the right people? For now I'll play along but I'll be sure to keep my distance, as there's still much I don't know.*

Quickly eating my food I looked to my side and saw Glave, the sword Nigh had given me. *Nigh, I'm sorry I was unable to help you, but maybe I'll be able to do something now, and help all of those from the south too.*

Stepping outside I walked forward. To my surprise I saw Smith in the distance as he smiled, "Hey Orion, long time no see, my friend."

"Smith? What are you doing here?"

"Well kiddo, for a long time I served King Alantt, but, you see I can't serve his brother. King Blake is a rather crazy old man, you know. So I was offered to help rebuild the south. Like I told you, I have a desire for knowledge and books, and so here I've been given access to the north's Library, which contains ancient books about alchemy, history, and all kinds of good books. Besides, how often does a blacksmith get the chance to join a revolution?" he said as he laughed.

"But Smith, does it not concern you that they're being led by Logan? I mean, he was a traitor, and he caused all of this."

"As far as I know, Orion, you're the leader here. Straif and Logan made that announcement a few days ago. We've all been a bit confused, but for now we've decided to trust in what they say. And about Logan, I'd heard that he did kill some knights back at the banquet and he didn't deny killing the crimson knights, but he explained to us that they were working for King Blake. After seeing what has become of the south, he sounds more reliable than most. Besides, most people were happy to hear that you would lead us. You see Nigh, your master is loved by all and they trust that his pupil will be a great leader like he was in the Blood War. In the end one must choose one evil over the other, and deal with the consequences, or so is the saying of the north, from what I have read in these books."

"Yeah, I guess nothing is so simple anymore. It's one evil or the other these days it seems. Smith, thanks, it means a lot that you and the others see me like a leader, but I've never even been to war. I haven't even agreed to lead this army, let alone have anything to do with it."

"It's a lot to take in, I know, but life always places us where we should be. You desire something so great that you've been given this chance. And son, you're not alone. We have many great minds among us, including Straif, Logan, and most of all myself. Believe it or not, we all believe a great deal in you."

"You know seeing you is pleasant. At least there's one person whose company I can enjoy around here. Well, if you don't mind, can you show me around?"

"Sure, come let's go, everyone will be happy to see that you have finally woken up. It has been a few days you know."

"I was out for a few days?"

"Yep, we had a medic take care of you, who is wonderful."

"Really? Who is it?"

"Astreya is her name. She's actually the one who brought the army together along with Logan. It's strange to think he's in charge but she's rather popular amongst the people."

"Really? I'd like to meet her. Her name sounds familiar. I think I've heard it before."

"Who knows, she seems loved by all so maybe you will meet her, but let's first get you to see everyone and maybe pass the library and take a look at some of the books they have there. I have to make sure that our leader is well educated."

"Sure, sounds like we have a busy day ahead."

"Well, what did you think it means to be a leader? It's not just fun and games. It requires a great mind, which I intend to make sure you acquire."

"So, I'm assuming we have a lot of preparation before we strike against the south?"

"Indeed, we do. See the leader in you is already thinking of the future strike."

"Yeah, it seems that way."

It was nice to see Smith here, yet surprising, but still I did not understand why someone like Logan would need me? He got rid of Nis so easily. Why couldn't he just lead this army or go and do it himself? It didn't make any sense why he needed me to lead his army. And now to add to the mix, there was a woman called Astreya who seemed just as important who I knew nothing of, yet I felt as if I had heard her name at some point.

Walking around the camp Smith pointed to each area as he explained, "There are the training grounds. We have many skilled soldiers from the south, east, and west. Many have defected from their kingdoms for various reasons, some were oppressed, others desire true freedom. Whatever the cause we have taken in all who wish to build a new world. You see, in this place we're free to believe in what we desire. We're free to practice alchemy or strive for new ideals."

"True freedom? So then who will truly be the leader here?"

"Well, young lad, like I said, what we are striving for is a new way of life, and so the people have decided who they desire to lead them. Logan took the time to explain to them the situation, and how you'd be able to lead them. He said you're a man of honor and integrity, that you possess not just great power but a good heart. After explaining to the people he gave everyone the chance to vote for who they desired to be their leader."

"So there were other candidates?"

"Yes, Astreya, Logan, and myself were the other candidates."

"But how, if you all want me to be the leader?"

"Well, we do yes, but we also weighed up the option that you may reject the offer and so we, too, made sure to show people our virtues. In the end, most people had heard about you from Logan for a long time, and from others who had seen you. Many know that you were born in the outside, as most people here. You see, every person here understands what you desire, and so they feel that you're perfect for the task. However, this title of leadership you shall claim if you decide to mount it shall not be the title of king, but rather a leader that represents his people."

"A leader that represents his people? I've never heard of such a title or position, but I'm interested to know how this system works."

"Well, the way it will work is that you shall have Logan, Astreya, and myself as advisors. Between the four of us we shall come up with plans and ways to improve our way of life. However, none of these plans can be set in motion without the people agreeing, therefore we shall establish a system where people can voice their thoughts, and this will help us reach out to those we would have never been able to otherwise."

"It seems complicated, but I like this idea. Show me more."

We walked into what once was the main palace of the north, which now laid in ruin. I was stunned to see that the walls had symbols carved all over them. They seemed familiar. I had seen them somewhere. But where? While thinking I remembered that when I was just a boy I'd seen them on the masked man, who had spoken with father, and later had met with Nigh and I before we entered the cave at the south.

"Hey Smith, these symbols, what are they?"

"These are old alchemy symbols. They've only been seen here. I've read many books pertaining alchemy but none had symbols such as these."

Walking closer I remembered the man's mask having one specific one that was made of a six-pointed star with numerous symbols around it. "Do you happen to know what this symbol means?"

Walking closer to the symbol Smith said, "Well, I believe Logan said that symbol is the symbol for human transmutation. He said it was used to bring the dead back to life."

"Is that so? And is that even possible?"

"Well, alchemy is a rather unknown subject for me, but I believe Logan said that it has never been attempted—only by one man."

"Who?"

"Samael, the Alchemist of the North."

"Logan once told me of this man. He said that he was betrayed by the Father of Alchemy, and that everyone died because they had killed his wife. He said that he drank the elixer of life and that there was another elixer that cursed the land and that's what brought about the Ashen."

"Yes that's true, but there's more to the story. I'm sure Logan didn't want to overwhelm you with so much history, but the Ashen predate back even further than the Ashen war. Long ago, in a land beyond this land, where there is just sand and stone, was a king, who by history was known as the king of old. I'm not sure how it happened but from that kingdom is where the Ashen curse originated from."

"Yes, I've heard of this from Nigh. He said there was a man who became the first king, wielding great power, and he ruled the lands. He then married a woman from far lands and fathered two children, who grew up with the desire to become like their father. After this the father had to send them away from the land because they had grown so fixated by this power that they began to wage war against one another. Afterwards they came to these lands and after years these kingdoms were built. Years later two men travelled back to the forgotten land. One called himself the Father of Alchemy and something happened that triggered the Ashen curse, or so I heard from Nigh.

"Well, Orion, I see you know much about your history, which is good, for history repeats itself. You said Nigh told you this? Well that's a surprise because that story is written in a book that only exists within this kingdom."

"Really? Well he said someone told him."

"It might be true, but maybe when we rescue him he can tell us more."

As Smith said this I thought back to the man who wore the mask, and how Nigh had been working with that man. I wondered what Nigh had been up to all this time. He apparently had ties to the north. *First the man whose mask had symbols that originate from the northland, and now he also knew a story that can only be read here. What does this all mean? How is Nigh connected to all of this? There is something I'm missing. I want to go back and explore that cave where Logan had all his research. I'll ask him to take me there, but first I'll continue to learn more about this place.*

Smith turned around and began to walk outside, "Well, let's go. I'll show you the library now." Walking outside he pointed to the tallest building in the area. "There, now we can go and see the library."

"That's enormous. It's even larger than the actual palace."

"Most people don't know this but the north wasn't like the other kingdoms. They were more focused on knowledge than politics, and so there was a king and queen, but merely for show and the need to have a face on the throne. But they, too, followed the path the people chose, always listening to their people's needs. It was the north who created the ideal of freedom for the people of this land."

"I see, and now we'll follow in their footsteps?"

"You say it as if it were bad. Orion, before you judge them and their past, educate yourself, and learn why people are who they are in history. You see, with time history is lost, changed, and can become a mere deception."

"Smith, I've already seen how deceptive people can be, so what would make anyone here less deceptive? I'll believe what I see for myself, and I'll make the decision on my own. I won't allow history and people's words to be what makes me choose a side."

"Such promising words, Orion," said the voice of a woman from behind me. Looking back I saw a woman with tanned skin, golden eyes, and long black hair, as she wore black armor with an alchemy symbol similar to the one of human transmutation, yet the stars had double the number of points."

"Who are you? And how do you know my name?"

"I can see so much of Nigh in your eyes. It seems he has done a fine job. He has made you into a man of worth. I am Astreya. Come, we have much to discuss, but first we ride to the southern villages as there is much Straif and myself have to show you, Orion."

Before I could say a word she walked away. I stood there thinking about how she knew Nigh. "Smith, do you know how she knows Nigh?"

"No, and Logan told me to never ask. Not even he knows, so I'd advise you to be careful with what you ask her. She isn't as kind as most with her words."

"What about the symbol she bears? It seems similar to the one of human transmutation, yet the star has 12 points."

"If I remember correctly that's the symbol of human deconstruction."

"Human deconstruction?"

"Yes, there are no books about it, but I asked Logan and that's all he said, yet he doesn't know much about it either it seemed."

"I see, well then I should get going. It seems the matter is urgent. When I come back we should take the time to go through some of those books,"

"Take your time, Orion, we have much ahead of us, young lad. This is just the beginning of your journey."

I quickly made my way back to the tent where I could see light, steel armor had been set aside for me, with a note that said, "Hope it fits."

Putting on the armor I grabbed Glave and made my way outside where the three of us met. Straif said, "Orion, we'll take a few men with us. It'll take us a while to reach the villages so bring extra clothes and anything else you may need."

I ran back inside and got extra clothes. Making my way outside we rode off soon after. While we rode I kept thinking how insane it was that I was now in the north with a rebel group who wanted to bring back the ideals of the kingdom that almost caused all the other kingdoms to be destroyed. But somehow this all made sense to me. Somehow it all seemed to tie in to this moment right now.

After riding for three days, only stopping to rest and eat, we finally reached what looked like villages in the distance. They sat in the middle of wheat fields, however something seemed wrong, as the sky was clouded by what looked like smoke. Astreya looked back at us all as she rode far ahead. "We're too late," she shouted, and when she did Straif made his way closer to her. I rode quickly to catch up with them but as I did we neared the entrance of the village. I could see that there was smoke coming from inside of the village. Smoke covered the air, ashes slowly covered everything, as the intense heat within the village could be felt upon my face. Looking around I saw fire burning within the village, entire homes engulfed in the flames. As the rubble fell I looked around for any signs of survivors, but everything seemed destroyed, burned to ashes. As we continued to go further in I began to smell what seemed like burning flesh, an all too familiar smell that reminded me of the night in my village.

Finally making my way deeper within the village I saw countless bodies piled up in what looked like a burning pit. "What the hell?" I screamed, quickly dismounting from the horse. I ran to where the bodies were. Here I saw only men had been burned. As I looked around the village I noticed what looked like more bodies. As I walked closer I saw a number of women had been chained to trees and beaten to death. As I looked up at the trees I witnessed the bodies of countless children as they hung lifeless. Walking closer, in disbelief I looked into their eyes. The children had suffered a great deal before they died. Their skin was pale as if they had been hung for hours, and their eyes had also been cut out. It seemed the mothers had been stripped naked and forced to watch from beneath the tree. They had been beaten to death, as their children suffocated, tied close to them so they could watch the life of their children fade before them. What cruelty, what madness. Who could have done this? Why had these people been killed in such a manner? Looking back at Straif I asked, "What the hell happened here? You said we were too late. You knew about this?"

Looking at me Straif said, "We'd received a message that this would be the next village but we weren't able to make it in time. We came here to save them but it seems they came before we were able to."

As Straif said these words, I heard men laughing. The sound came from behind one of the houses. Walking to the back of the house I saw a woman being raped by men as they held the husband and her daughter on the ground. Enraged, I pulled out my sword, but as I did I looked around and witnessed what looked like a hundred men come from the tree line.

The men were wearing the armor from the south. As the leader walked closer, I recalled his face: he was one of the knights I had trained with, in the past.

"What the hell is the meaning of this?" I asked with anger.

As the knights laughed, the one I knew said, "Orion, you have no place to speak. You're a traitor. We're here on official orders, as these peasants are heretics, and they're a waste."

"A waste, you say? That will cost you your life, Doran."

"You remember my name? I feel honored."

Straif and Astreya made their way to where I was as Straif said desperately, "Orion, we're outnumbered here. We must go."

Astreya looked at me and said, "No ordinary man can avenge these people. You see that woman being defiled by those men? You see that man suffering with his child, as his wife is raped in front of him? You see all these countless lives lost to such horrible ways? Orion, only you can change this. Call him upon your wrath and avenge their deaths. Give them back what they deserve. Give them the vengeance of death."

Astreya's words echoed in my head. Every word she said made me feel even more angry, "I shall kill them, I shall kill them all," I whispered to myself, as Doran pointed at me, and said, "Look men, Orion is afraid."

"You will all die here, you bastards!" I screamed at the top of my lungs, and as I did I felt a great pain inside my chest, a pain as if something were trying to break free from within me. Falling to my knees from the pain, I felt my chest break open as the black gauntlet of Nis tore its way through. I saw a black symbol appear before me, which seemed to have rotating rings that stopped as if unlocking something, and as if made of glass it cracked and then disappeared. The pain was unbearable. All of my body felt as if it were being cut to shreds. Everyone looked shocked, except for Astreya. The men screamed at the top of their lungs, "What the fuck is he?"

I felt their hearts beating faster and the fear within their minds consume them. Soon my body began to feel a sensation of euphoria, as their fear fed my anger. I felt invincible. My body felt more alive than it had ever felt, and as they ran in all directions I slowly stood from the ground. The black gauntlet was no longer there, but the hole in my chest was, as I walked forward. Doran quivered in fear, "What the hell are you?"

With a smile, I looked at Doran. "I am death, destroyer of worlds." I could hear voices in my head as they echoed, "Kill them all, make them pay for what they have done, release me."

"Nis, kill them, destroy everything."

"It shall be done, my king."

A black fog came from within my chest as Nis slowly took form, his armor as black as the abyss. He stood taller than any man. His armor was hard to see as the smoke covered it, but it was fitting for a giant.

The ground turned black and from the blackness rose even more knights that looked like Nis. The men ran and as they ran in fear I saw Nis chase them, cutting their arms, their legs, every part of them. The sight of their deaths brought a smile to my face, as Doran fell to his knees. Nis knew I desired to kill him myself, so Doran was left kneeling for me. Walking forward I heard as he begged for his life. Doran whispered, "Please, maker, please don't let this demon kill me like this, please."

Placing my hand on his forehead the only words I could think of were, "You believe that you deserve salvation? Doran, go back to the south and tell your king that I shall come to take the crown from the cradle of his shoulders. Tell him that I, the true king, shall take for myself the crown he bears." As I said this I placed my finger on his forehead, and as I did so I said to Nis, "Once he gives this message to the king, I want you to kill him, and leave the king a message for me." A hand reached out from within me, as it carved a symbol on Doran's head, "His death is sealed."

Doran cried, as he closed his eyes. Walking away I said, "Your death is certain. May you suffer every second of it."

Walking towards the woman, I looked to the side where I saw my reflection on one of the shields the men from the south carried. Looking closer, I could see my face was pale, my hair white, and my left eye pitch black. In disbelief, I walked closer, "What? It can't be? What is this?" Holding the shield to my face I saw my skin slowly change back to its normal color, my chest healed completely, but my left eye did not change. Touching it I felt as if there was something deep within. As the vision blurred on my left eye, I slowly lost all sight there. "How could this happen?" The sound of a little girl crying came to my attention. Looking back I could still see the little girl on the ground. Dropping the shield, I saw everyone was still paralyzed by what had happened. Closing my left eye I walked towards the crying child. Making my way to where the woman who had been raped laid, I could see that her throat had been cut before I was able to save her and that the father's head had been smashed in. The little girl's eyes had been cut out as she cried in pain. "There, there, little girl, I'm here to save you," I said as I touched her, but she moved away in fear begging for her life, as if confused. "Please mister, please don't kill me, please."

To see this innocent child suffer this much broke my heart. To see tears come from her eyes with blood from her wounds made me realize that there is little we can do as humans to save one another, that the innocent are caught in these senseless struggles and pay dearly for those who are evil. Looking around all the men had been killed. Straif and Astreya stood waiting to come closer. Straif looked afraid still, but Astreya looked like she had something else in mind. I knew that what I had done may have been the work of a beast, but there was no other choice, not for those men, only death.

Holding the little girl in my hands, I slowly cleaned her bloody tears from her face as she shook in fear. I heard her call out beneath her breath in fear. "Mom, dad, where are you? Mom? I'm scared. Dad? Please answer me."

There were no words I could say to alleviate the pain this child felt. As my anger subsided I saw Nis walking towards me as he slowly disappeared, and as he did, somehow I saw one of the many Nis's staring at me, different from the rest, as he extended his hand. This one reminded me of the one in the forest, and for some reason I felt different with this one. Before disappearing I faintly saw what looked like a face show itself. It seemed familiar, but I wasn't sure of who it could be. All I saw last were the bright blue eyes fade.

Looking back at the little girl, I said, "My name is Orion. Tell me, what is your name?"

"It hurts, mister. My eyes hurt. Where's my mom and dad? I can't see! Those men, they were here! AHHHHHHH."

Confused and in pain she began to scramble around, "Mommmyyyyy!"

I held her tight and said, "Sorry, but they're gone. I'm so sorry."

When I said those words her lips began to tremble as she cried once again. Ripping a piece of cloth from beneath my armor I tied it around her eyes. "I'm sorry, but we must take care of you. You're badly wounded, so we must tend to your wounds."

"Ourania, that's the name my mom gave me," she said crying.

Walking closer to me Astreya said, "Orion, sometimes one must become a necessary evil to achieve a greater good."

I closed my eyes while holding Ourania as I repeated her words in my head, "One must become a necessary evil to achieve a greater good."

Opening my eyes I looked at her, as I said, "I shall be what you seek, I shall be the king without a crown, I shall lead the armies of the north against all and any who stand in the path of freedom and justice, I shall be the sword of justice this world needs, even if that sword is one of evil."

With a smile Astreya said, "Then as of today all shall hail Orion, the Crownless King."

# EPILOGUE

"Gabriel, awaken, thou journey is far from over."
I could hear the voice of Codex calling to me, but all I could see was blackness. Then suddenly I found myself staring at an enormous kingdom, withered and torn apart by war. It was hard to see as the gusting winds blew sand around the kingdom. Walked forward, my foot stumbled upon a shield and as I looked down the winds parted the sand. Beneath my feet I saw countless bodies of knights with spears and swords scattered through the land. Looking back at the kingdom I saw the castle built of pure black steel, slowly reconstructing itself as if time itself were turning back. Within moments, the largest kingdom I had ever seen stood before me. Then the bodies slowly stood and as if a great battle were playing backwards, spears were withdrawn from the bodies of the knights, swords returned to their sheaths, and knights ran backwards into the distance. Great flaming boulders reconstructed themselves and took back to the skies, where they landed back at their catapults. Once again the knights found themselves in formation. Looking up at the sky I witnessed the smoke clear up and the sand storm slowly fade. Looking at the gate of the kingdom again stood a large man with ragged clothes bearing a crown and an enormous sword that equaled his size. With the sword impaled on the ground it seemed as if he stood in place ready for battle.

"Codex, tell me, is what I'm seeing here real? Where am I? This doesn't look like the land you had taken me to, to watch over the nine."

"The nine do not belong to one time and place. Here before you stands the first of the nine, the last true king known to man, the King of Old."

"The King of Old? He's the one Logan spoke of?"

"Indeed, he was the beginning of the end."

"He's the one who brought about the end? But how? I thought it was a war in the land we stood before?"

"All ends have a root. Before you tread any further peer into his eyes. Only a kin may stand before him."

Walking forward, I was impressed to see that he was even taller than I thought, and his body full of scars. His hair of ash fell down his shoulders as his blackened eyes looked down upon me. Looking into his eyes, I felt a sense of emptiness, nothingness, as if I were in a void. Closing his eyes, the entire world around me disintegrated, as if turning to dust. To my surprise, I found myself once again in the kingdom of the south.

"What happened?"

"You are still unworthy of the truth. You must seek the true kin."

"Unworthy? What kin?"

"Follow the voice of pain."

In the distance I heard screams. Looking around the south was covered with guards, but none could see me. Walking toward the screaming voice, I began to feel as if someone were stabbing my body. Falling to the ground, I heard another voice, a cynical voice whispering to me.

"How does it feel, traitor? So many called you the Abyssal Knight, and now here you are, dying like a worm."

Opening my eyes, I saw Nigh, chained in a cell as a man heated a knife and slowly cut deep inside his abdomen. Screaming in agony Nigh pulled on the chains, but the more he screamed the more the man tortured him.

"It is time Gabriel. It is time for you to understand true despair."

As Codex uttered those words, my body was drawn to Nigh's, as memories came crashing into me. Once again, like with Orion, I found myself in another's body, but this time I felt a heavy burden, an inner void, similar to that of the King of Old. And with my final thoughts pain took over me. I looked at the man's face of enjoyment, as he bit his lip while cutting me.

"Nigh, don't worry, the king has ordered you to suffer, not die."

Gasping for air I looked up. "This man, I'd cut him to pieces if I could, damned Logan. I'll kill him when I free myself from this hell."

"Such hate in those eyes, but worry not, Nigh. I must go now. I hope you get some rest, as tomorrow will be a long day."

The man slowly walked away, as my vision blurred. Looking down I saw that little blood had been spilled, yet he had cut me deep.

"It seems he was sealing my wounds rapidly so I wouldn't bleed to death. Orion, I believe no matter what I must endure that you're the worthy king of this land. I know that you shall free this land, Orion. I believe in you. Closing my eyes, I felt the comfort of silence, as my body went cold. Feeling soft hands touch my face I slowly looked up. To my surprise I could not believe it was her.

"You?"

"Shhh. I'm here to help you my love."

Jorge Vazquez is a Military Service Member and author. He is the youngest of three, and was raised in Miami, Florida. Growing up in the city of Miami, it was evident that Jorge had a passion for writing and creating stories. By the age of ten, unfortunate events led him to live in a shelter, along with his older brother, Jesus Vazquez. Despite their young age, the two brothers continued to pursue a better future. With hard work and dedication they made it past many of life's obstacles, however Jorge was fortunate that his brother sacrificed his dreams to provide them both with the means to survive. In the midst of the difficult times, Jorge kept true to his passion with writing, and was finally recognized for his talents at the age of 18 as a senior in high school. Upon graduation he continued to go to college with the desire for a better life, where he exposed himself to the military. Having met those who served the U.S. he decided to not only be a writer but also a soldier. While in the Army, he continued to write for his brothers in arms, ultimately leading him to writing his first novel, in the name of all those who had helped him through the struggles of life.

Lightning Source UK Ltd.
Milton Keynes UK
UKOW04f1416240915

259194UK00003B/90/P